CW01424746

BIRDS OF PREY
Seven Sardonic Stories

BIRDS OF PREY

Seven Sardonic Stories

Daphne du Maurier • Salman Rushdie
Christopher Ondaatje • Edgar Allan Poe
Julian Barnes • Richard Burton

Introduction by
Margaret Drabble

RARE BOOKS AND BERRY
2010

First published in 2010 by

Rare Books and Berry
High Street, Porlock, Minehead, Somerset TA24 8PU

www.rarebooksandberry.co.uk

Introduction © Margaret Drabble 2010

'The Birds' © Daphne du Maurier, 1952. Reproduced with permission of
Curtis Brown Group Ltd, London on behalf of the Chichester Partnership.

'The Firebird's Nest' © 1997, Salman Rushdie. Reproduced by permission of
The Wylie Agency (UK) Ltd. All rights reserved.

From 'Flaubert's Parrot' by Julian Barnes, published by Jonathan Cape.
Reprinted by permission of The Random House Group Ltd.

Brief extract of biography of Julian Barnes © Julian Barnes, 2005.
As appeared in *The Guardian*.

'The Devil Bird' and 'The White Crow' © Christopher Ondaatje, 2009.

A CIP catalogue record for this title is available from the British Library

ISBN 978-0-9557119-9-2

Designed and typeset in Minion at Alacrity, Sandford, Somerset

Printed and bound by
The Cromwell Press Group, Wiltshire

CONDITIONS OF SALE

All rights reserved. No part of this publication may be reproduced,
stored in a retrieval system, or transmitted in any form or by any means,
electronic, mechanical, photocopying, recording or otherwise, without
the prior permission of the publisher.

This book is sold subject to the condition that it shall not, by way of trade
or otherwise, be lent, re-sold, hired out or otherwise circulated without the
publisher's prior consent in any form of binding or cover other than that in
which it is published and without a similar condition including this
condition being imposed on the subsequent purchaser.

Contents

Photographic Acknowledgements

Daphne du Maurier: Hans Wild – Time & Life Pictures/Getty Images
Julian Barnes: Steve Pyke – Getty Images
Edgar Allan Poe: Time & Life Pictures/Getty Images
Salman Rushdie: Joe Kohen – WireImage/Getty Images
Christopher Ondaatje: Thad Peterson – The Ondaatje Foundation
Christopher Ondaatje and President J.R. Jayawardene
– The Ondaatje Foundation

Introduction

THIS COLLECTION of tales and anecdotes has a powerful linking theme which makes the whole more than the sum of its parts, all of which are interesting in their own right. Short stories come in many forms, and serve many purposes – they can deliver a short sharp shock or a devastating punch-line, they can evoke a place or atmosphere, or they can take us into the mind of a single narrator. Here we have a variety of styles, but all connected to a single subject – the subject of birds. In England we tend to think of birds as friendly little garden visitors, and we put out crumbs and nuts for them. These birds are more menacing. With one ironic exception, Flaubert's parrot, they are Gothic birds, birds of prey, dangerous birds, devouring birds, killer birds.

Daphne du Maurier's story 'The Birds' is a classic of its genre, terrifying, suggestive, allegorical, and it portrays birds, all birds, from the little finches and robins to the gathering armies of gulls, hawks, buzzards and falcons, as a menace to man. Its theme is fear. Edgar Allan Poe's hypnotic incantatory poem 'The Raven' is equally sinister. Ravens have always had a bad name as birds of death and the battlefield, and this poem adds a gloomy indoor antiquarian raven's cry to an old tradition. This is not the kind of bird you would like to find sitting in your study.

In all countries, superstitions attach themselves to birds, which are often seen as portents or bad omens, and some of these tales have a distinctly oriental menace. Salman Rushdie's 'The Firebird's Nest' and Christopher Ondaatje's two tales of misfortune and disaster both spring from a tradition of folklore and fear where a western or westernised observer enters or strays into a mysterious world which operates by different rules: the wife in Rushdie's story has a very narrow escape, and a worse fate is suffered by the woman journalist in Ondaatje's 'The White Crow'. Witchcraft and demonology are palpable. Richard Burton's story is also full of a more sporting but equally destructive violence, in which, as in du Maurier's tale, birds show a sinister capacity for organised attack. These writers remind us that most of our British birds, in normal times, are shy and elusive. The mythical phoenix and the firebird do not visit our shores, and our crows and ravens are not as menacing now as they were in medieval times.

It is different in other lands. I remember that, on my only visit to India, I was astonished when a large bird swooped from the sky and snatched the roast chicken from my plate as I sat harmlessly taking a little lunch outdoors in Calcutta. I thought it was a kite, but, reading Burton's story, I wonder if it was perhaps a crow. Foreign birds, as these stories illustrate, are not to be trusted. This was, for me, a deeply oriental moment.

The word 'oriental' must be used with care these days, but both Christopher Ondaatje and Richard Burton are distinguished as travellers and adventurers who bring to their tales an authentic sense of other cultures, colourful landscapes, and a touch of distinctively Gothic orientalism. Burton produced in 1885-8 a celebrated translation of *The Arabian Nights Entertainments*, one of the world's great treasure houses of stories, and the tradition of story-telling as an oral and conversational art is well captured in this volume. Tall stories, believe-it-or-not stories, fairy stories have a long history, and the short story is a form that liberates the writer from a literal realism. Real characters and legendary characters mingle, mixing fact with fiction. It is enough to suggest. There is no need to explain.

Julian Barnes's parrot belongs to a totally different genre, although his poor badly stuffed fowl is just as vividly evoked, and his tone too is first-person and conversational. But his narrator's aim is not to reinforce or relay or create myth, but to explore and expose it. The story which inspired Barnes's novel, Flaubert's *Un Coeur Simple*, published in 1877, is one of the greatest stories in the realist tradition, which tells how Félicité, a poor, aged and faithful domestic servant, comes to believe that her parrot is the Holy Ghost. Flaubert, who was also something of an orientalist, wonderfully and surprisingly combines a tender and prosaic account of her delusion with an unobtrusive symbolism. The oriental parrot, Loulou, stranded in northern Normandy, is not as alarming as a devil bird or a firebird, but she is just as powerful an image, and Barnes gives her a new meaning and a new life.

As this volume illustrates, the short story, in prose or verse, is a flexible form in which a writer can say much more than appears at first sight. Cumulatively, this interesting selection makes us think again about real birds, symbolic birds, mythical birds, and leaves us with a memory of strange and haunting landscapes where the unexpected and the unexplained prevail.

MARGARET DRABBLE
January 2010

Daphne du Maurier

1907-1989

DAPHNE DU MAURIER'S terrifying short story 'The Birds' was first published in 1952 in a collection called *The Apple Tree*. The story was inspired shortly after World War II when the author watched a man on the Cornish coast ploughing his field while seagulls wheeled and dived above him. The story was later made into a film directed by Alfred Hitchcock in 1963.

Curiously, in material revealed by her biographer Margaret Forster, du Maurier had secretly discussed her own unusual attitude to her ambiguous sexuality. She was, she said, convinced that she was really two completely different people: a loving wife and mother; and the lover – a force driven by a definite male energy which was the fiendish power behind her creative writing.

Daphne du Maurier was born in London on 13 May 1907 and was the second of three daughters of the actor-manager Sir Gerald du Maurier and the actress Muriel Beaumont. She married Lieutenant-General Sir Frederick 'Boy' Browning and had two daughters and a son. She was created a Dame of the British Empire in 1969. Her first novel *The Loving Spirit* was published in 1931, but the novel *Rebecca* is by far her most famous literary creation. Other important works include *Jamaica Inn*, *Frenchman's Creek*, *Hungry Hill*, *My Cousin Rachel* and *The King's General* – the last of which was the first novel she wrote at Menabilly, the house she leased for many years from the Rashleigh family in Cornwall. Her husband Lieutenant-General Browning died in 1965, after which she moved from Menabilly to Kilmarth, near Par, which later became the setting for one of her last novels, *The House on the Strand*. She died on 19th April 1989 at her home in Cornwall. Her body was cremated and her ashes scattered at Kilmarth.

The Birds

O N DECEMBER the third the wind changed overnight and
it was winter. Until then the autumn had been mellow,
soft. The leaves had lingered on the trees, golden red, and
the hedgerows were still green. The earth was rich where the
plough had turned it.

Nat Hocken, because of a war-time disability, had a pension and
did not work full-time at the farm. He worked three days a week,
and they gave him the lighter jobs: hedging, thatching, repairs to
the farm buildings.

Although he was married, with children, his was a solitary
disposition; he liked best to work alone. It pleased him when he
was given a bank to build up, or a gate to mend at the far end of
the peninsula, where the sea surrounded the farm land on either
side. Then, at midday, he would pause and eat the pasty that his
wife had baked for him, and sitting on the cliff's edge would watch
the birds. Autumn was best for this, better than spring. In spring
the birds flew inland, purposeful, intent; they knew where they
were bound, the rhythm and ritual of their life brooked no delay.
In autumn those that had not migrated overseas but remained to
pass the winter were caught up in the same driving urge, but
because migration was denied them followed a pattern of their
own. Great flocks of them came to the peninsula, restless, uneasy,
spending themselves in motion; now wheeling, circling in the sky,
now settling to feed on the rich new-turned soil, but even when
they fed it was as though they did so without hunger, without
desire. Restlessness drove them to the skies again.

Black and white, jackdaw and gull, mingled in strange partnership, seeking some sort of liberation, never satisfied, never still. Flocks of starlings, rustling like silk, flew to fresh pasture, driven by the same necessity of movement, and the smaller birds, the finches and the larks, scattered from tree to hedge as if compelled.

Nat watched them, and he watched the sea-birds too. Down in the bay they waited for the tide. They had more patience. Oyster-catchers, redshank, sanderling, and curlew watched by the water's edge; as the slow sea sucked at the shore and then withdrew, leaving the strip of seaweed bare and the shingle churned, the sea-birds raced and ran upon the beaches. Then that same impulse to flight seized upon them too. Crying, whistling, calling, they skimmed the placid sea and left the shore. Make haste, make speed, hurry and begone: yet where, and to what purpose? The restless urge of autumn, unsatisfying, sad, had put a spell upon them and they must flock, and wheel, and cry; they must spill themselves of motion before winter came.

Perhaps, thought Nat, munching his pasty by the cliff's edge, a message comes to the birds in autumn, like a warning. Winter is coming. Many of them perish. And like people who, apprehensive of death before their time, drive themselves to work or folly, the birds do likewise.

The birds had been more restless than ever this fall of the year, the agitation more marked because the days were still. As the tractor traced its path up and down the western hills, the figure of the farmer silhouetted on the driving-seat, the whole machine and the man upon it would be lost momentarily in the great cloud of wheeling, crying birds. There were many more than usual, Nat was sure of this. Always, in autumn, they followed the plough, but not in great flocks like these, nor with such clamour.

Nat remarked upon it, when hedging was finished for the day. 'Yes,' said the farmer, 'there are more birds about than usual; I've noticed it too. And daring, some of them, taking no notice of the tractor. One or two gulls came so close to my head this afternoon

I thought they'd knock my cap off! As it was, I could scarcely see what I was doing, when they were overhead and I had the sun in my eyes. I have a notion the weather will change. It will be a hard winter. That's why the birds are restless.'

Nat, tramping home across the fields and down the lane to his cottage, saw the birds still flocking over the western hills, in the last glow of the sun. No wind, and the grey sea calm and full. Campion in bloom yet in the hedges, and the air mild. The farmer was right, though, and it was that night the weather turned. Nat's bedroom faced east. He woke just after two and heard the wind in the chimney. Not the storm and bluster of a sou'westerly gale, bringing the rain, but east wind, cold and dry. It sounded hollow in the chimney, and a loose slate rattled on the roof. Nat listened, and he could hear the sea roaring in the bay. Even the air in the small bedroom had turned chill: a draught came under the skirting of the door, blowing upon the bed. Nat drew the blanket round him, leant closer to the back of his sleeping wife, and stayed wakeful, watchful, aware of misgiving without cause.

Then he heard the tapping on the window. There was no creeper on the cottage walls to break loose and scratch upon the pane. He listened, and the tapping continued until, irritated by the sound, Nat got out of bed and went to the window. He opened it, and as he did so something brushed his hand, jabbing at his knuckles, grazing the skin. Then he saw the flutter of the wings and it was gone, over the roof, behind the cottage.

It was a bird, what kind of bird he could not tell. The wind must have driven it to shelter on the sill.

He shut the window and went back to bed, but feeling his knuckles wet put his mouth to the scratch. The bird had drawn blood. Frightened, he supposed, and bewildered, the bird, seeking shelter, had stabbed at him in the darkness. Once more he settled himself to sleep.

Presently the tapping came again, this time more forceful, more insistent, and now his wife woke at the sound, and turning in the bed said to him, 'See to the window, Nat, it's rattling.'

'I've already seen to it,' he told her, 'there's some bird there, trying to get in. Can't you hear the wind? It's blowing from the east, driving the birds to shelter.'

'Send them away,' she said, 'I can't sleep with that noise.'

He went to the window for the second time, and now when he opened it there was not one bird upon the sill but half a dozen; they flew straight into his face, attacking him.

He shouted, striking out at them with his arms, scattering them; like the first one, they flew over the roof and disappeared. Quickly he let the window fall and latched it.

'Did you hear that?' he said. 'They went for me. Tried to peck my eyes.' He stood by the window, peering into the darkness, and could see nothing. His wife, heavy with sleep, murmured from the bed.

'I'm not making it up,' he said, angry at her suggestion. 'I tell you the birds were on the sill, trying to get into the room.'

Suddenly a frightened cry came from the room across the passage where the children slept.

'It's Jill,' said his wife, roused at the sound, sitting up in bed. 'Go to her, see what's the matter.'

Nat lit the candle, but when he opened the bedroom door to cross the passage the draught blew out the flame.

There came a second cry of terror, this time from both children, and stumbling into their room he felt the beating of wings about him in the darkness. The window was wide open. Through it came the birds, hitting first the ceiling and the walls, then swerving in mid-flight, turning to the children in their beds.

'It's all right, I'm here,' shouted Nat, and the children flung themselves, screaming, upon him, while in the darkness the birds rose and dived and came for him again.

'What is it, Nat, what's happened?' his wife called from the further bedroom, and swiftly he pushed the children through the door to the passage and shut it upon them, so that he was alone now, in their bedroom, with the birds.

He seized a blanket from the nearest bed, and using it as a weapon flung it to right and left about him in the air. He felt the thud of bodies, heard the fluttering of wings, but they were not yet defeated, for again and again they returned to the assault, jabbing his hands, his head, the little stabbing beaks sharp as a pointed fork. The blanket became a weapon of defence; he wound it about his head, and then in greater darkness beat at the birds with his bare hands. He dared not stumble to the door and open it, lest in doing so the birds should follow him.

How long he fought with them in the darkness he could not tell, but at last the beating of the wings about him lessened and then withdrew, and through the density of the blanket he was aware of light. He waited, listened; there was no sound except the fretful crying of one of the children from the bedroom beyond. The fluttering, the whirring of the wings had ceased.

He took the blanket from his head and stared about him. The cold grey morning light exposed the room. Dawn, and the open window, had called the living birds; the dead lay on the floor. Nat gazed at the little corpses, shocked and horrified. They were all small birds, none of any size; there must have been fifty of them lying there upon the floor. There were robins, finches, sparrows, blue tits, larks and bramblings, birds that by nature's law kept to their own flock and their own territory, and now, joining one with another in their urge for battle, had destroyed themselves against the bedroom walls, or in the strife had been destroyed by him. Some had lost feathers in the fight, others had blood, his blood, upon their beaks.

Sickened, Nat went to the window and stared out across his patch of garden to the fields.

It was bitter cold, and the ground had all the hard black look of frost. Not white frost, to shine in the morning sun, but the black frost that the east wind brings. The sea, fiercer now with the turning tide, white-capped and steep, broke harshly in the bay. Of the birds there was no sign. Not a sparrow chattered in the hedge beyond the garden gate, no early missel-thrush or blackbird pecked on the grass for worms. There was no sound at all but the east wind and the sea.

Nat shut the window and the door of the small bedroom, and went back across the passage to his own. His wife sat up in bed, one child asleep beside her, the smaller in her arms, his face bandaged. The curtains were tightly drawn across the window, the candles lit. Her face looked garish in the yellow light. She shook her head for silence.

'He's sleeping now,' she whispered, 'but only just. Something must have cut him, there was blood at the corner of his eyes. Jill said it was the birds. She said she woke up, and the birds were in the room.'

His wife looked up at Nat, searching his face for confirmation. She looked terrified, bewildered, and he did not want her to know that he was also shaken, dazed almost, by the events of the past few hours.

'There are birds in there,' he said, 'dead birds, nearly fifty of them. Robins, wrens, all the little birds from hereabouts. It's as though a madness seized them, with the east wind.' He sat down on the bed beside his wife, and held her hand. 'It's the weather,' he said, 'it must be that, it's the hard weather. They aren't the birds, maybe, from here around. They've been driven down, from up country.'

'But Nat,' whispered his wife, 'it's only this night that the weather turned. There's been no snow to drive them. And they can't be hungry yet. There's food for them, out there, in the fields.'

'It's the weather,' repeated Nat. 'I tell you, it's the weather.'

His face too was drawn and tired, like hers. They stared at one another for a while without speaking.

'I'll go downstairs and make a cup of tea,' he said.

The sight of the kitchen reassured him. The cups and saucers, neatly stacked upon the dresser, the table and chairs, his wife's roll of knitting on her basket chair, the children's toys in a corner cupboard.

He knelt down, raked out the old embers and relit the fire. The glowing sticks brought normality, the steaming kettle and the brown teapot comfort and security. He drank his tea, carried a cup up to his wife. Then he washed in the scullery, and, putting on his boots, opened the back door.

The sky was hard and leaden, and the brown hills that had gleamed in the sun the day before looked dark and bare. The east wind, like a razor, stripped the trees, and the leaves, crackling and dry, shivered and scattered with the wind's blast. Nat stubbed the earth with his boot. It was frozen hard. He had never known a change so swift and sudden. Black winter had descended in a single night.

The children were awake now. Jill was chattering upstairs and young Johnny crying once again. Nat heard his wife's voice, soothing, comforting. Presently they came down. He had breakfast ready for them, and the routine of the day began.

'Did you drive away the birds?' asked Jill, restored to calm because of the kitchen fire, because of day, because of breakfast.

'Yes, they've all gone now,' said Nat. 'It was the east wind brought them in. They were frightened and lost, they wanted shelter.'

'They tried to peck us,' said Jill. 'They went for Johnny's eyes.'

'Fright made them do that,' said Nat. 'They didn't know where they were, in the dark bedroom.'

'I hope they won't come again,' said Jill. 'Perhaps if we put bread for them outside the window they will eat that and fly away.'

She finished her breakfast and then went for her coat and hood, her school books and her satchel. Nat said nothing, but his wife looked at him across the table. A silent message passed between them.

'I'll walk with her to the bus,' he said, 'I don't go to the farm today.'

And while the child was washing in the scullery he said to his wife, 'Keep all the windows closed, and the doors too. Just to be on the safe side. I'll go to the farm. Find out if they heard anything

19

in the night.' Then he walked with his small daughter up the lane. She seemed to have forgotten her experience of the night before. She danced ahead of him, chasing the leaves, her face whipped with the cold and rosy under the pixie hood.

'Is it going to snow, Dad?' she said. 'It's cold enough.'

He glanced up at the bleak sky, felt the wind tear at his shoulders.

'No,' he said, 'it's not going to snow. This is a black winter, not a white one.'

All the while he searched the hedgerows for the birds, glanced over the top of them to the fields beyond, looked to the small wood above the farm where the rooks and jackdaws gathered. He saw none.

The other children waited by the bus-stop, muffled, hooded like Jill, the faces white and pinched with cold.

Jill ran to them, waving. 'My Dad says it won't snow,' she called, 'it's going to be a black winter.'

She said nothing of the birds. She began to push and struggle with another little girl. The bus came ambling up the hill. Nat saw her on to it, then turned and walked back towards the farm. It was not his day for work, but he wanted to satisfy himself that all was well. Jim, the cowman, was clattering in the yard.

'Boss around?' asked Nat.

'Gone to market,' said Jim. 'It's Tuesday, isn't it?'

He clumped off round the corner of a shed. He had no time for Nat. Nat was said to be superior. Read books, and the like. Nat had forgotten it was Tuesday. This showed how the events of the preceding night had shaken him. He went to the back door of the farm-house and heard Mrs Trigg singing in the kitchen, the wireless making a background to her song.

'Are you there, missus?' called out Nat.

She came to the door, beaming, broad, a good-tempered woman.

'Hullo, Mr Hocken,' she said. 'Can you tell me where this cold is coming from? Is it Russia? I've never seen such a change. And it's going on, the wireless says. Something to do with the Arctic circle.'

'We didn't turn on the wireless this morning,' said Nat. 'Fact is, we had trouble in the night.'

'Kiddies poorly?'

'No …' He hardly knew how to explain it. Now, in daylight, the battle of the birds would sound absurd.

He tried to tell Mrs Trigg what had happened, but he could see from her eyes that she thought his story was the result of a nightmare.

'Sure they were real birds,' she said, smiling, 'with proper feathers and all? Not the funny-shaped kind, that the men see after closing hours on a Saturday night?'

'Mrs Trigg,' he said, 'there are fifty dead birds, robins, wrens, and such, lying low on the floor of the children's bedroom. They went for me; they tried to go for young Johnny's eyes.'

Mrs Trigg stared at him doubtfully.

'Well there, now,' she answered, 'I suppose the weather brought them. Once in the bedroom, they wouldn't know where they were to. Foreign birds maybe, from that Arctic circle.'

'No,' said Nat, 'they were the birds you see about here every day.'

'Funny thing,' said Mrs Trigg, 'no explaining it, really. You ought to write up and ask the *Guardian*. They'd have some answer for it. Well, I must be getting on.'

She nodded, smiled, and went back into the kitchen.

Nat, dissatisfied, turned to the farm-gate. Had it not been for those corpses on the bedroom floor, which he must now collect and bury somewhere, he would have considered the tale exaggeration too.

Jim was standing by the gate.

'Had any trouble with the birds?' asked Nat.

'Birds? What birds?'

'We got them up our place last night. Scores of them, came in the children's bedroom Quite savage they were.'

21

'Oh?' It took time for anything to penetrate Jim's head. 'Never heard of birds acting savage,' he said at length. 'They get tame, like, sometimes. I've seen them come to the windows for crumbs.'

'These birds last night weren't tame.'

'No? Cold maybe. Hungry. You put out some crumbs.'

Jim was no more interested than Mrs Trigg had been. It was, Nat thought, like air-raids in the war. No one down this end of the country knew what the Plymouth folk had seen and suffered. You had to endure something yourself before it touched you. He walked back along the lane and crossed the stile to his cottage. He found his wife in the kitchen with young Johnny.

'See anyone?' she asked.

'Mrs Trigg and Jim,' he answered. 'I don't think they believed me. Anyway, nothing wrong up there.'

'You might take the birds away,' she said. 'I daren't go into the room to make the beds until you do. I'm scared.'

'Nothing to scare you now,' said Nat. 'They're dead, aren't they?'

He went up with a sack and dropped the stiff bodies into it, one by one. Yes, there were fifty of them, all told. Just the ordinary common birds of the hedgerow, nothing as large even as a thrush. It must have been fright that made them act the way they did. Blue tits, wrens, it was incredible to think of the power of their small beaks, jabbing at his face and hands the night before. He took the sack out into the garden and was faced now with a fresh problem. The ground was too hard to dig. It was frozen solid, yet no snow had fallen, nothing had happened in the past hours but the coming of the east wind. It was unnatural, queer. The weather prophets must be right. The change was something connected with the Arctic circle.

The wind seemed to cut him to the bone as he stood there, uncertainly, holding the sack. He could see the white-capped seas breaking down under in the bay. He decided to take the birds to the shore and bury them.

When he reached the beach below the headland he could scarcely stand, the force of the east wind was so strong. It hurt to draw breath, and his bare hands were blue. Never had he known such cold, not in all the bad winters he could remember. It was low tide. He crunched his way over the shingle to the softer sand and then, his back to the wind, ground a pit in the sand with his heel. He meant to drop the birds into it, but as he opened up the sack the force of the wind carried them, lifted them, as though in flight again, and they were blown away from him along the beach, tossed like feathers, spread and scattered, the bodies of the fifty frozen birds. There was something ugly in the sight He did not like it. The dead birds were swept away from him by the wind.

'The tide will take them when it turns,' he said to himself.

He looked out to sea and watched the crested breakers, combing green. They rose stiffly, curled, and broke again, and because it was ebb tide the roar was distant, more remote, lacking the sound and thunder of the flood.

Then he saw them. The gulls. Out there, riding the seas.

What he had thought at first to be the white caps of the waves were gulls. Hundreds, thousands, tens of thousands. They rose and fell in the trough of the seas, heads to the wind, like a mighty fleet at anchor, waiting on the tide. To eastward, and to the west, the gulls were there. They stretched as far as his eye could reach, in close formation, line upon line. Had the sea been still they would have covered the bay like a white cloud, head to head, body packed to body. Only the east wind, whipping the sea to breakers, hid them from the shore.

Nat turned, and leaving the beach climbed the steep path home. Someone should know of this. Someone should be told. Something was happening, because of the east wind and the weather, that he did not understand. He wondered if he should go to the call-box by the bus-stop and ring up the police. Yet what could they do? What could anyone do? Tens and thousands of gulls riding the sea there, in the bay, because of storm, because of hunger. The police would think him mad, or drunk, or take the statement from him with great calm. 'Thank you. Yes, the matter has already been reported. The hard weather is driving the birds inland in great numbers.' Nat looked about him. Still no sign of any other bird. Perhaps the cold had sent them all from up country? As he drew near to the cottage his wife came to meet him, at the door. She called to him, excited. 'Nat,' she said, 'it's on the wireless. They've just read out a special news bulletin. I've written it down.'

'What's on the wireless?' he said.

'About the birds,' she said. 'It's not only here, it's everywhere. In London, all over the country. Something has happened to the birds.'

Together they went into the kitchen. He read the piece of paper lying on the table.

'Statement from the Home Office at eleven a.m. today. Reports from all over the country are coming in hourly about the vast quantity of birds flocking above towns, villages, and outlying districts, causing obstruction and damage and even attacking individuals. It is thought that the Arctic air stream, at present covering the British Isles, is causing birds to migrate south in immense numbers, and that intense hunger may drive these birds to attack human beings. Householders are warned to see to their windows, doors, and chimneys, and to take reasonable precautions for the safety of their children. A further statement will be issued later.'

A kind of excitement seized Nat; he looked at his wife in triumph.

'There you are,' he said, 'let's hope they'll hear that at the farm. Mrs Trigg will know it wasn't any story. It's true. All over the country. I've been telling myself all morning there's something wrong. And just now, down on the beach, I looked out to sea and there are gulls, thousands of them, tens of thousands, you couldn't put a pin between their heads, and they're all out there, riding on the sea, waiting.'

'What are they waiting for, Nat?' she asked.

He stared at her, then looked down again at the piece of paper.

'I don't know,' he said slowly. 'It says here the birds are hungry.'

He went over to the drawer where he kept his hammer and tools.

'What are you going to do, Nat?'

'See to the windows and the chimneys too, like they tell you.'

'You think they would break in, with the windows shut? Those sparrows and robins and such? Why, how could they?'

He did not answer. He was not thinking of the robins and the sparrows. He was thinking of the gulls…

He went upstairs and worked there the rest of the morning, boarding the windows of the bedrooms, filling up the chimney bases. Good job it was his free day and he was not working at the farm. It reminded him of the old days, at the beginning of the war. He was not married then, and he had made all the blackout boards for his mother's house in Plymouth. Made the shelter too. Not that it had been of any use, when the moment came. He wondered if they would take these precautions up at the farm. He doubted it. Too easy-going, Harry Trigg and his missus. Maybe they'd laugh at the whole thing. Go off to a dance or a whist drive.

'Dinner's ready.' She called him, from the kitchen.

'All right. Coming down.'

He was pleased with his handiwork. The frames fitted nicely over the little panes and at the base of the chimneys.

When dinner was over and his wife was washing up, Nat switched on the one o'clock news. The same announcement was repeated, the one which she had taken down during the morning, but the news bulletin enlarged upon it. 'The flocks of birds have caused dislocation in all areas,' read the announcer, 'and in London the sky was so dense at ten o'clock this morning that it seemed as if the city was covered by a vast black cloud.

'The birds settled on roof-tops, on window ledges and on chimneys. The species included blackbird, thrush, the common house-sparrow, and, as might be expected in the metropolis, a vast quantity of pigeons and starlings, and that frequenter of the London river, the black-headed gull. The sight has been so unusual that traffic came to a standstill in many thoroughfares, work was abandoned in shops and offices, and the streets and pavements were crowded with people standing about to watch the birds.'

Various incidents were recounted, the suspected reason of cold and hunger stated again, and warnings to householders repeated. The announcer's voice was smooth and suave. Nat had the impression that this man, in particular, treated the whole business as he would an elaborate joke. There would be others like him, hundreds of them, who did not know what it was to struggle in darkness with a flock of birds. There would be parties tonight in London, like the ones they gave on election nights. People standing about, shouting and laughing, getting drunk. 'Come and watch the birds!'

Nat switched off the wireless. He got up and started work on the kitchen windows. His wife watched him, young Johnny at her heels.

'What, boards for down here too?' she said. 'Why, I'll have to light up before three o'clock. I see no call for boards down here.'

'Better be sure than sorry,' answered Nat. 'I'm not going to take any chances.'

'What they ought to do,' she said, 'is to call the army out and shoot the birds. That would soon scare them off.'

'Let them try,' said Nat. 'How'd they set about it?'

'They have the army to the docks,' she answered, 'when the dockers strike. The soldiers go down and unload the ships.'

'Yes,' said Nat, 'and the population of London is eight million or more. Think of all the buildings, all the flats, and houses. Do you think they've enough soldiers to go round shooting birds from every roof?'

'I don't know. But something should be done. They ought to do something.'

Nat thought to himself that 'they' were no doubt considering the problem at that very moment, but whatever 'they' decided to do in London and the big cities would not help the people here, three hundred miles away. Each householder must look after his own.

'How are we off for food?' he said.

'Now, Nat, whatever next?'

'Never mind. What have you got in the larder?'

'It's shopping day tomorrow, you know that. I don't keep uncooked food hanging about, it goes off. Butcher doesn't call till the day after. But I can bring back something when I go in tomorrow.'

Nat did not want to scare her. He thought it possible that she might not go to town tomorrow. He looked in the larder for himself, and in the cupboard where she kept her tins. They would do, for a couple of days. Bread was low.

'What about the baker?'

'He comes tomorrow too.'

He saw she had flour. If the baker did not call she had enough to bake one loaf.

'We'd be better off in the old days,' he said, 'when the women baked twice a week, and had pilchards salted, and there was food for a family to last a siege, if need be.'

'I've tried the children with tinned fish, they don't like it,' she said.

Nat went on hammering the boards across the kitchen windows. Candles. They were low in candles too. That must be another thing she meant to buy tomorrow. Well, it could not be helped. They must go early to bed tonight. That was, if …

He got up and went out of the back door and stood in the garden, looking down towards the sea. There had been no sun all day, and now, at barely three o'clock, a kind of darkness had already come, the sky sullen, heavy, colourless like salt. He could hear the vicious sea drumming on the rocks. He walked down the path, half-way to the beach. And then he stopped. He could see the tide had turned. The rock that had shown in mid-morning was now covered, but it was not the sea that held his eyes. The gulls had risen. They were circling, hundreds of them, thousands of them, lifting their wings against the wind. It was the gulls that made the darkening of the sky. And they were silent. They made not a sound. They just went on soaring and circling, rising, falling, trying their strength against the wind.

Nat turned. He ran up the path, back to the cottage.

'I'm going for Jill,' he said. 'I'll wait for her, at the bus-stop.'

'What's the matter?' asked his wife. 'You've gone quite white.'

'Keep Johnny inside,' he said. 'Keep the door shut. Light up now, and draw the curtains.'

'It's only just gone three,' she said.

'Never mind. Do what I tell you.'

He looked inside the toolshed, outside the back door. Nothing there of much use. A spade was too heavy, and a fork no good. He took the hoe. It was the only possible tool, and light enough to carry.

He started walking up the lane to the bus-stop, and now and again glanced back over his shoulder.

The gulls had risen higher now, their circles were broader, wider, they were spreading out in huge formation across the sky.

He hurried on; although he knew the bus would not come to the top of the hill before four o'clock he had to hurry. He passed no one on the way. He was glad of this. No time to stop and chatter.

At the top of the hill he waited. He was much too soon. There was half an hour still to go. The east wind came whipping across the fields from the higher ground. He stamped his feet and blew upon his hands. In the distance he could see the clay hills, white and clean, against the heavy pallor of the sky. Something black rose from behind them, like a smudge at first, then widening, becoming deeper, and the smudge became a cloud, and the cloud divided again into five other clouds, spreading north, east, south and west, and they were not clouds at all; they were birds. He watched them travel across the sky, and as one section passed overhead, within two or three hundred feet of him, he knew from their speed, they were bound inland, up country, they had no business with the people here on the peninsula. They were rooks, crows, jackdaws, magpies, jays, all birds that usually preyed upon the smaller species; but this afternoon they were bound on some other mission.

'They've been given the towns,' thought Nat, 'they know what they have to do. We don't matter so much here. The gulls will serve for us. The others go to the towns.'

He went to the call-box, stepped inside and lifted the receiver. The exchange would do. They would pass the message on.

'I'm speaking from Highway,' he said, 'by the bus-stop. I want to report large formations of birds travelling up country. The gulls are also forming in the bay.'

'All right,' answered the voice, laconic, weary.

'You'll be sure and pass this message on to the proper quarter?'

'Yes ... yes ...' Impatient now, fed-up. The buzzing note resumed.

'She's another,' thought Nat, 'she doesn't care. Maybe she's had to answer calls all day. She hopes to go to the pictures tonight. She'll squeeze some fellow's hand, and point up at the sky, and say, "Look at all them birds!" She doesn't care.'

The bus came lumbering up the hill. Jill climbed out and three or four other children. The bus went on towards the town.

'What's the hoe for, Dad?'

They crowded around him, laughing, pointing.

'I just brought it along,' he said. 'Come on now, let's get home. It's cold, no hanging about. Here, you. I'll watch you across the fields, see how fast you can run.'

He was speaking to Jill's companions who came from different families, living in the council houses. A short cut would take them to the cottages.

'We want to play a bit in the lane,' said one of them.

'No, you don't. You go off home, or I'll tell your mammy.'

They whispered to one another, round-eyed, then scuttled off across the fields. Jill stared at her father, her mouth sullen.

'We always play in the lane,' she said.

'Not tonight, you don't,' he said. 'Come on now, no dawdling.'

He could see the gulls now, circling the fields, coming in towards the land. Still silent. Still no sound.

'Look, Dad, look over there, look at all the gulls.'

'Yes. Hurry, now.'

'Where are they flying to? Where are they going?'

'Up country, I dare say. Where it's warmer.'

He seized her hand and dragged her after him along the lane.

'Don't go so fast. I can't keep up.'

The gulls were copying the rooks and crows. They were spreading out in formation across the sky. They headed, in bands of thousands, to the four compass points.

'Dad, what is it? What are the gulls doing?'

They were not intent upon their flight, as the crows, as the jackdaws had been. They still circled overhead. Nor did they fly so high. It was as though they waited upon some signal. As though some decision had yet to be given. The order was not clear.

'Do you want me to carry you, Jill? Here, come pick-a-back.'

This way he might put on speed; but he was wrong. Jill was heavy. She kept slipping. And she was crying too. His sense of urgency, of fear, had communicated itself to the child.

'I wish the gulls would go away. I don't like them. They're coming closer to the lane.'

He put her down again. He started running, swinging Jill after him. As they went past the farm turning he saw the farmer backing his car out of the garage. Nat called to him.

'Can you give us a lift?' he said.

'What's that?'

Mr Trigg turned in the driving seat and stared at them. Then a smile came to his cheerful, rubicund face.

'It looks as though we're in for some fun,' he said. 'Have you seen the gulls? Jim and I are going to take a crack at them. Everyone's gone bird crazy, talking of nothing else. I hear you were troubled in the night. Want a gun?'

Nat shook his head.

The small car was packed. There was just room for Jill, if she crouched on top of petrol tins on the back seat.

'I don't want a gun,' said Nat, 'but I'd be obliged if you'd run Jill home. She's scared of the birds.'

He spoke briefly. He did not want to talk in front of Jill.

'OK,' said the farmer, 'I'll take her home. Why don't you stop behind and join the shooting match? We'll make the feathers fly.'

Jill climbed in, and turning the car the driver sped up the lane. Nat followed after. Trigg must be crazy. What use was a gun against a sky of birds?

Now Nat was not responsible for Jill he had time to look about him. The birds were circling still, above the fields. Mostly herring gull, but the black-headed gull amongst them. Usually they kept apart. Now they were united. Some bond had brought them together. It was the black-backed gull that attacked the smaller birds, and even new-born lambs, so he'd heard. He'd never seen it done. He remembered this now, though, looking above him in the sky. They were coming in towards the farm. They were circling lower in the sky, and the black-backed gulls were to the front, the black-backed gulls were leading. The farm, then, was their target. They were making for the farm.

Nat increased his pace towards his own cottage. He saw the farmer's car turn and come back along the lane. It drew up beside him with a jerk.

'The kid has run inside,' said the farmer. 'Your wife was watching for her. Well, what do you make of it? They're saying in town the Russians have done it. The Russians have poisoned the birds.'

'How could they do that?' asked Nat.

'Don't ask me. You know how stories get around. Will you join my shooting match?'

'No, I'll get along home. The wife will be worried else.'

'My missus says if you could eat gull, there'd be some sense in it,' said Trigg, 'we'd have roast gull, baked gull, and pickle 'em into the bargain. You wait until I let off a few barrels into the brutes. That'll scare 'em.'

'Have you boarded your windows?' asked Nat.

'No. Lot of nonsense. They like to scare you on the wireless. I've had more to do today than to go round boarding up my windows.'

'I'd board them now, if I were you.'

'Garn. You're windy. Like to come to our place to sleep?'

'No, thanks all the same.'

'All right. See you in the morning. Give you a gull breakfast.'

The farmer grinned and turned his car to the farm entrance.

Nat hurried on. Past the hide wood, past the old barn, and then across the stile to the remaining field.

As he jumped the stile he heard the whirr of wings. A black-backed gull dived down at him from the sky, missed, swerved in flight, and rose to dive again. In a moment it was joined by others, six, seven, a dozen, black-backed and herring mixed. Nat dropped his hoe. The hoe was useless. Covering his head with his arms he ran towards the cottage. They kept coming at him from the air, silent save for the beating wings. The terrible, fluttering wings He could feel the blood on his hands, his wrists, his neck. Each stab of a swooping beak tore his flesh If only he could keep them from his eyes. Nothing else mattered. He must keep them from his eyes. They had not learnt yet how to cling to a shoulder, how to rip clothing, how to dive in mass upon the head, upon the body. But with each dive, with each attack, they became bolder. And they had no thought for themselves. When they dived low and missed, they crashed, bruised and broken, on the ground. As Nat ran he stumbled, kicking their spent bodies in front of him.

He found the door, he hammered upon it with his bleeding hands. Because of the boarded windows no light shone. Everything was dark.

'Let me in,' he shouted, 'it's Nat. Let me in.'

He shouted loud to make himself heard above the whirr of the gulls' wings.

Then he saw the gannet, poised for the dive, above him in the sky. The gulls circled, retired, soared, one with another, against the wind. Only the gannet remained. One single gannet, above him in the sky. The wings folded suddenly to its body. It dropped like a stone. Nat screamed, and the door opened. He stumbled across the threshold, and his wife threw her weight against the door.

They heard the thud of the gannet as it fell.

His wife dressed his wounds. They were not deep. The backs of his hands had suffered most, and his wrists. Had he not worn a cap they would have reached his head. As to the gannet … the gannet could have split his skull.

The children were crying, of course. They had seen the blood on their father's hands.

'It's all right now,' he told them. 'I'm not hurt. Just a few scratches. You play with Johnny, Jill. Mammy will wash these cuts.'

He half shut the door to the scullery, so that they could not see. His wife was ashen. She began running water from the sink.

'I saw them overhead,' she whispered. 'They began collecting just as Jill ran in with Mr Trigg. I shut the door fast, and it jammed. That's why I couldn't open it at once, when you came.'

'Thank God they waited for me,' he said. 'Jill would have fallen at once. One bird alone would have done it.'

Furtively, so as not to alarm the children, they whispered together, as she bandaged his hands and the back of his neck.

'They're flying inland,' he said, 'thousands of them. Rooks, crows, all the bigger birds. I saw them from the bus-stop. They're making for the towns.

'But what can they do, Nat?'

'They'll attack. Go for everyone out in the streets. Then they'll try the windows, the chimneys.'

'Why don't the authorities do something? Why don't they get the army, get machine-guns, anything?'

'There's been no time. Nobody's prepared. We'll hear what they have to say on the six o'clock news.'

Nat went back into the kitchen, followed by his wife. Johnny was playing quietly on the floor. Only Jill looked anxious.

'I can hear the birds,' she said. 'Listen, Dad.'

Nat listened. Muffled sounds came from the windows, from the door. Wings brushing the surface, sliding, scraping, seeking a way of entry. The sound of many bodies, pressed together, shuffling on the sills. Now and again came a thud, a crash, as some bird dived and fell. 'Some of them will kill themselves that way,' he thought, 'but not enough. Never enough.'

'All right,' he said aloud, 'I've got boards over the windows, Jill. The birds can't get in.'

He went and examined all the windows. His work had been thorough. Every gap was closed. He would make extra certain, however. He found wedges, pieces of old tin, strips of wood and metal, and fastened them at the sides to reinforce the boards. His hammering helped to deafen the sound of the birds, the shuffling, the tapping, and more ominous – he did not want his wife or the children to hear it – the splinter of cracked glass.

'Turn on the wireless,' he said, 'let's have the wireless.'

This would drown the sound also. He went upstairs to the bed-rooms and reinforced the windows there. Now he could hear the birds on the roof, the scraping of claws, a sliding, jostling sound.

He decided they must sleep in the kitchen, keep up the fire, bring down the mattresses and lay them out on the floor. He was afraid of the bedroom chimneys. The boards he had placed at the chimney bases might give way. In the kitchen they would be safe, because of the fire. He would have to make a joke of it. Pretend to the children they were playing at camp. If the worst happened, and the birds forced an entry down the bedroom chimneys, it would be hours, days perhaps, before they could break down the doors. The birds would be imprisoned in the bedrooms. They could do no harm there. Crowded together, they would stifle and die.

He began to bring the mattresses downstairs. At sight of them his wife's eyes widened in apprehension. She thought the birds had already broken in upstairs.

'All right,' he said cheerfully, 'we'll all sleep together in the kitchen tonight. More cosy here by the fire. Then we shan't be worried by those silly old birds tapping at the windows.'

He made the children help him rearrange the furniture, and he took the precaution of moving the dresser, with his wife's help, across the window. It fitted well. It was an added safeguard. The mattresses could now be lain, one beside the other, against the wall where the dresser had stood.

'We're safe enough now,' he thought, 'we're snug and tight, like an air-raid shelter. We can hold out. It's just the food that worries me. Food, and coal for the fire. We've enough for two or three days, not more. By that time...'

No use thinking ahead as far as that. And they'd be giving directions on the wireless. People would be told what to do. And now, in the midst of many problems, he realized that it was dance music only coming over the air. Not Children's Hour, as it should have been. He glanced at the dial. Yes, they were on the Home Service all right. Dance records. He switched to the Light pro-gramme. He knew the reason. The usual programmes had been abandoned. This only happened at exceptional times. Elections, and such. He tried to remember if it had happened in the war, during the heavy raids on London. But of course. The BBC was not stationed in London during the war. The programmes were broadcast from other, temporary quarters. 'We're better off here,' he thought, 'we're better off here in the kitchen, with the windows and the doors boarded, than they are up in the towns. Thank God we're not in the towns.'

At six o'clock the records ceased. The time signal was given. No matter if it scared the children, he must hear the news. There was a pause after the pips. Then the announcer spoke. His voice was solemn, grave. Quite different from midday.

'This is London,' he said. 'A National Emergency was proclaimed at four o'clock this afternoon. Measures are being taken to safe-guard the lives and property of the population, but it must be understood that these are not easy to effect immediately, owing to the unforeseen and unparalleled nature of the present crisis. Every householder must take precautions to his own building, and where several people live together, as in flats and apartments, they must unite to do the utmost they can to prevent entry. It is absolutely imperative that every individual stays indoors tonight, and that no one at all remains on the streets, or roads, or anywhere without doors. The birds, in vast numbers, are attacking anyone on sight, and have already begun an assault upon buildings; but these, with due care, should be impenetrable. The population is asked to remain calm, and not to panic. Owing to the exceptional nature of the emergency, there will be no further transmission from any broadcasting station until seven a.m. tomorrow.'

They played the National Anthem. Nothing more happened. Nat switched off the set. He looked at his wife. She stared back at him.

'What's it mean?' said Jill. 'What did the news say?'

'There won't be any more programmes tonight,' said Nat. 'There's been a breakdown at the BBC.'

'Is it the birds?' asked Jill. 'Have the birds done it?'

'No,' said Nat, 'it's just that everyone's very busy, and then of course they have to get rid of the birds, messing everything up, in the towns. Well, we can manage without the wireless for one evening.'

'I wish we had a gramophone,' said Jill, 'that would be better than nothing.'

She had her face turned to the dresser, backed against the windows. Try as they did to ignore it, they were all aware of the shuffling, the stabbing, the persistent beating and sweeping of wings.

'We'll have supper early,' suggested Nat, 'something for a treat. Ask Mammy. Toasted cheese, eh? Something we all like?'

He winked and nodded at his wife. He wanted the look of dread, of apprehension, to go from Jill's face.

He helped with the supper, whistling, singing, making as much clatter as he could, and it seemed to him that the shuffling and the tapping were not so intense as they had been at first. Presently he went up to the bedrooms and listened, and he no longer heard the jostling for place upon the roof.

'They've got reasoning powers,' he thought, 'they know it's hard to break in here. They'll try elsewhere. They won't waste their time with us.'

Supper passed without incident, and then, when they were clearing away, they heard a new sound, droning, familiar, a sound they all knew and understood.

His wife looked up at him, her face alight. 'It's planes,' she said, 'they're sending out planes after the birds. That's what I said they ought to do, all along. That will get them. Isn't that gunfire? Can't you hear guns?'

It might be gun-fire, out at sea. Nat could not tell. Big naval guns might have an effect upon the gulls out at sea, but the gulls were inland now. The guns couldn't shell the shore, because of the population.

'It's good, isn't it,' said his wife, 'to hear the planes?'

And Jill, catching her enthusiasm, jumped up and down with Johnny. 'The planes will get the birds. The planes will shoot them.'

Just then they heard a crash about two miles distant, followed by a second, then a third. The droning became more distant, passed away out to sea.

'What was that?' asked his wife. 'Were they dropping bombs on the birds?'

'I don't know,' answered Nat, 'I don't think so.'

He did not want to tell her that the sound they had heard was the crashing of aircraft. It was, he had no doubt, a venture on the part of the authorities to send out reconnaissance forces, but they might have known the venture was suicidal. What could aircraft do against birds that flung themselves to death against propeller and fuselage, but hurtle to the ground themselves? This was being tried now, he supposed, over the whole country. And at a cost. Someone high up had lost his head.

'Where have the planes gone, Dad?' asked Jill.

'Back to base,' he said. 'Come on, now, time to tuck down for bed.'

It kept his wife occupied, undressing the children before the fire, seeing to the bedding, one thing and another, while he went round the cottage again, making sure that nothing had worked loose. There was no farther drone of aircraft, and the naval guns had ceased. 'Waste of life and effort,' Nat said to himself. 'We can't destroy enough of them that way. Cost too heavy. There's always gas. Maybe they'll try spraying with gas, mustard gas. We'll be warned first, of course, if they do. There's one thing, the best brains of the country will be on to it tonight.'

Somehow the thought reassured him. He had a picture of scientists, naturalists, technicians, and all those chaps they called the back-room boys, summoned to a council; they'd be working on the problem now. This was not a job for the government, for the chiefs-of-staff – they would merely carry out the orders of the scientists.

'They'll have to be ruthless,' he thought. 'Where the trouble's worst they'll have to risk more lives, if they use gas. All the livestock, too, and the soil – all contaminated. As long as everyone doesn't panic. That's the trouble. People panicking, losing their heads. The BBC was right to warn us of that.'

Upstairs in the bedrooms all was quiet. No further scraping and stabbing at the windows. A lull in battle. Forces regrouping. Wasn't that what they called it, in the old war-time bulletins? The wind hadn't dropped, though. He could still hear it, roaring in the chimneys. And the sea breaking down on the shore. Then he remembered the tide. The tide would be on the turn. Maybe the lull in battle was because of the tide. There was some law the birds obeyed, and it was all to do with the east wind and the tide.

He glanced at his watch. Nearly eight o'clock. It must have gone high water an hour ago. That explained the lull: the birds attacked with the flood tide. It might not work that way inland, up country, but it seemed as if it was so this way on the coast. He reckoned the time limit in his head. They had six hours to go, without attack. When the tide turned again, around one-twenty in the morning, the birds would come back…

There were two things he could do. The first to rest, with his wife and the children, and all of them snatch what sleep they could, until the small hours. The second to go out, see how they were faring at the farm, see if the telephone was still working there, so that they might get news from the exchange.

He called softly to his wife, who had just settled the children. She came half-way up the stairs and he whispered to her.

'You're not to go,' she said at once, 'you're not to go and leave me alone with the children. I can't stand it.'

Her voice rose hysterically. He hushed her, calmed her.

'All right,' he said, 'all right. I'll wait till morning. And we'll get the wireless bulletin then too, at seven. But in the morning, when the tide ebbs again, I'll try for the farm, and they may let us have bread and potatoes, and milk too.'

His mind was busy again, planning against emergency. They would not have milked, of course, this evening. The cows would be standing by the gate, waiting in the yard, with the household inside, battened behind boards, as they were here at the cottage.

That is, if they had time to take precautions. He thought of the farmer, Trigg, smiling at him from the car. There would have been no shooting party, not tonight.

The children were asleep. His wife, still clothed, was sitting on her mattress. She watched him, her eyes nervous.

'What are you going to do?' she whispered.

He shook his head for silence. Softly, stealthily, he opened the back door and looked outside.

It was pitch dark. The wind was blowing harder than ever, coming in steady gusts, icy, from the sea. He kicked at the step outside the door. It was heaped with birds. There were dead birds everywhere. Under the windows, against the walls. These were the suicides, the divers, the ones with broken necks. Wherever he looked he saw dead birds. No trace of the living. The living had flown seaward with the turn of the tide. The gulls would be riding the seas now, as they had done in the forenoon.

In the far distance, on the hill where the tractor had been two days before, something was burning. One of the aircraft that had crashed; the fire, fanned by the wind, had set light to a stack.

He looked at the bodies of the birds, and he had a notion that if he heaped them, one upon the other, on the window sills they would make added protection for the next attack. Not much, perhaps, but something. The bodies would have to be clawed at, pecked, and dragged aside, before the living birds gained purchase on the sills and attacked the panes. He set to work in the darkness. It was queer; he hated touching them. The bodies were still warm and bloody. The blood matted their feathers. He felt his stomach turn, but he went on with his work. He noticed, grimly, that every window-pane was shattered. Only the boards had kept the birds from breaking in. He stuffed the cracked panes with the bleeding bodies of the birds.

When he had finished he went back into the cottage. He barricaded the kitchen door, made it doubly secure. He took off his bandages, sticky with the birds' blood, not with his own cuts, and put on fresh plaster.

His wife had made him cocoa and he drank it thirstily. He was very tired.

'All right,' he said, smiling, 'don't worry. We'll get through.'

He lay down on his mattress and closed his eyes. He slept at once. He dreamt uneasily, because through his dreams there ran a thread of something forgotten. Some piece of work, neglected, that he should have done. Some precaution that he had known well but had not taken, and he could not put a name to it in his dreams. It was connected in some way with the burning aircraft and the stack upon the hill. He went on sleeping, though; he did not awake. It was his wife shaking his shoulder that awoke him finally.

'They've begun,' she sobbed, 'they've started this last hour, I can't listen to it any longer, alone. There's something smelling bad too, something burning.'

Then he remembered. He had forgotten to make up the fire. It was smouldering, nearly out. He got up swiftly and lit the lamp.

The hammering had started at the windows and the doors, but it was not that he minded now. It was the smell of singed feathers. The smell filled the kitchen. He knew at once what it was. The birds were coming down the chimney, squeezing their way down to the kitchen range.

He got sticks and paper and put them on the embers, then reached for the can of paraffin.

'Stand back,' he shouted to his wife, 'we've got to risk this.'

He threw the paraffin on to the fire. The flame roared up the pipe, and down upon the fire fell the scorched, blackened bodies of the birds.

The children woke, crying. 'What is it?' said Jill. 'What's happened?'

Nat had no time to answer. He was raking the bodies from the chimney, clawing them out on to the floor. The flames still roared, and the danger of the chimney catching fire was one he had to take. The flames would send away the living birds from the chimney top. The lower joint was the difficulty, though. This was choked with the smouldering helpless bodies of the birds caught by fire. He scarcely heeded the attack on the windows and the door: let them beat their wings, break their beaks, lose their lives, in the attempt to force an entry into his home. They would not break in. He thanked God he had one of the old cottages, with small windows, stout walls. Not like the new council houses. Heaven help them up the lane, in the new council houses.

'Stop crying,' he called to the children. 'There's nothing to be afraid of, stop crying.'

He went on raking at the burning, smouldering bodies as they fell into the fire.

'This'll fetch them,' he said to himself, 'the draught and the flames together. We're all right, as long as the chimney doesn't catch. I ought to be shot for this. It's all my fault. Last thing I should have made up the fire. I knew there was something.'

Amid the scratching and tearing at the window boards came the sudden homely striking of the kitchen clock. Three a.m. A little

41

more than four hours yet to go. He could not be sure of the exact time of high water. He reckoned it would not turn much before half past seven, twenty to eight.

'Light up the primus,' he said to his wife. 'Make us some tea, and the kids some cocoa. No use sitting around doing nothing.'

That was the line. Keep her busy, and the children too. Move about, eat, drink; always best to be on the go.

He waited by the range. The flames were dying. But no more blackened bodies fell from the chimney. He thrust his poker up as far as it could go and found nothing. It was clear. The chimney was clear. He wiped the sweat from his forehead.

'Come on now, Jill,' he said, 'bring me some more sticks. We'll have a good fire going directly.' She wouldn't come near him, though. She was staring at the heaped singed bodies of the birds.

'Never mind them,' he said, 'we'll put those in the passage when I've got the fire steady.'

The danger of the chimney was over. It could not happen again, not if the fire was kept burning day and night.

'I'll have to get more fuel from the farm tomorrow,' he thought. 'This will never last. I'll manage, though. I can do all that with the ebb tide. It can be worked, fetching what we need, when the tide's turned. We've just got to adapt ourselves, that's all.'

They drank tea and cocoa and ate slices of bread and Bovril. Only half a loaf left, Nat noticed. Never mind though, they'd get by.

'Stop it,' said young Johnny, pointing to the windows with his spoon, 'stop it, you old birds.'

'That's right,' said Nat, smiling, 'we don't want the old beggars, do we? Had enough of 'em.'

They began to cheer when they heard the thud of the suicide birds.

'There's another, Dad,' cried Jill, 'he's done for.'

'He's had it,' said Nat, 'there he goes, the blighter.'

This was the way to face up to it. This was the spirit. If they could keep this up, hang on like this until seven, when the

42

first news bulletin came through, they would not have done too badly.

'Give us a fag,' he said to his wife. 'A bit of a smoke will clear away the smell of the scorched feathers.'

'There's only two left in the packet,' she said. 'I was going to buy you some from the Co-op.'

'I'll have one,' he said, 't'other will keep for a rainy day.'

No sense trying to make the children rest. There was no rest to be got while the tapping and the scratching went on at the windows. He sat with one arm round his wife and the other round Jill, with Johnny on his mother's lap and the blankets heaped about them on the mattress.

'You can't help admiring the beggars,' he said, 'they've got persistence. You'd think they'd tire of the game, but not a bit of it.'

Admiration was hard to sustain. The tapping went on and on and a new rasping note struck Nat's ear, as though a sharper beak than any hitherto had come to take over from its fellows. He tried to remember the names of birds, he tried to think which species would go for this particular job. It was not the tap of the woodpecker. That would be light and frequent. This was more serious, because if it continued long the wood would splinter as the glass had done. Then he remembered the hawks. Could the hawks have taken over from the gulls? Were there buzzards now upon the sills, using talons as well as beaks? Hawks, buzzards, kestrels, falcons – he had forgotten the birds of prey. He had forgotten the gripping power of the birds of prey. Three hours to go, and while they waited the sound of the splintering wood, the talons tearing at the wood.

Nat looked about him, seeing what furniture he could destroy to fortify the door. The windows were safe, because of the dresser. He was not certain of the door. He went upstairs, but when he reached the landing he paused and listened. There was a soft patter on the floor of the children's bedroom. The birds had broken through ... He put his ear to the door. No mistake. He could hear the rustle of wings, and the light patter as they searched the floor. The other bedroom was still clear. He went into it and began bringing out the furniture, to pile at the head of the stairs should the door of the children's bedroom go. It was a preparation. It might never be needed. He could not stack the furniture against the door, because it opened inward. The only possible thing was to have it at the top of the stairs.

'Come down, Nat, what are you doing?' called his wife

'I won't be long,' he shouted. 'Just making everything shipshape up here.'

He did not want her to come; he did not want her to hear the pattering of the feet in the children's bedroom, the brushing of those wings against the door.

At five-thirty he suggested breakfast, bacon and fried bread, if only to stop the growing look of panic in his wife's eyes and to calm the fretful children. She did not know about the birds upstairs. The bedroom, luckily, was not over the kitchen. Had it been so she could not have failed to hear the sound of them, up there, tapping the boards. And the silly, senseless thud of the suicide birds, the death-and-glory boys, who flew into the bedroom, smashing their heads against the walls. He knew them of old, the herring gulls. They had no brains. The black-backs were different, they knew what they were doing. So did the buzzards, the hawks...

He found himself watching the clock, gazing at the hands that went so slowly round the dial. If his theory was not correct, if the attack did not cease with the turn of the tide, he knew they were beaten. They could not continue through the long day without air, without rest, without more fuel, without ... his mind raced. He knew there were so many things they needed to withstand siege. They were not fully prepared. They were not ready. It might be that it would be safer in the towns after all. If he could get a message through, on the farm telephone, to his cousin, only a short journey by train up country, they might be able to hire a car. That would be quicker – hire a car between tides...

His wife's voice, calling his name, drove away the sudden, desperate desire for sleep.

'What is it? What now?' he said sharply.

'The wireless,' said his wife. 'I've been watching the clock. It's nearly seven.'

'Don't twist the knob,' he said, impatient for the first time, 'it's on the Home where it is. They'll speak from the Home.'

They waited. The kitchen clock struck seven. There was no sound. No chimes, no music. They waited until a quarter past, switching to the Light. The result was the same. No news bulletin came through.

'We've heard wrong,' he said, 'they won't be broadcasting until eight o'clock.'

They left it switched on, and Nat thought of the battery, wondered how much power was left in it. It was generally recharged when his wife went shopping in the town. If the battery failed they would not hear the instructions.

'It's getting light,' whispered his wife, 'I can't see it, but I can feel it. And the birds aren't hammering so loud.'

She was right. The rasping, tearing sound grew fainter every moment. So did the shuffling, the jostling for place upon the step, upon the sills. The tide was on the turn. By eight there was no sound at all. Only the wind. The children, lulled at last by the stillness, fell asleep. At half past eight Nat switched the wireless off.

'What are you doing? We'll miss the news,' said his wife.

'There isn't going to be any news,' said Nat. 'We've got to depend upon ourselves.'

He went to the door and slowly pulled away the barricades. He drew the bolts, and kicking the bodies from the step outside the door breathed the cold air. He had six working hours before him, and he knew he must reserve his strength for the right things, not waste it in any way. Food, and light, and fuel; these were the necessary things. If he could get them in sufficiency, they could endure another night.

He stepped into the garden, and as he did so he saw the living birds. The gulls had gone to ride the sea, as they had done before; they sought sea food, and the buoyancy of the tide, before they returned to the attack. Not so the land birds. They waited and watched. Nat saw them, on the hedgerows, on the soil, crowded in the trees, outside in the field, line upon line of birds, all still, doing nothing.

He went to the end of his small garden. The birds did not move. They went on watching him.

'I've got to get food,' said Nat to himself, 'I've got to go to the farm to find food.'

He went back to the cottage. He saw to the windows and the doors. He went upstairs and opened the children's bedroom. It was empty, except for the dead birds on the floor. The living were out there, in the garden, in the fields. He went downstairs.

'I'm going to the farm,' he said.

His wife clung to him. She had seen the living birds from the open door.

'Take us with you,' she begged, 'we can't stay here alone. I'd rather die than stay here alone.'

He considered the matter. He nodded.

'Come on, then,' he said, 'bring baskets, and Johnny's pram. We can load up the pram.'

They dressed against the biting wind, wore gloves and scarves. His wife put Johnny in the pram. Nat took Jill's hand.

'The birds' she whimpered, 'they're all out there, in the fields.'

'They won't hurt us,' he said, 'not in the light.'

They started walking across the field towards the sole, and the birds did not move. They waited, their heads turned to the wind.

When they reached the turning to the farm, Nat stopped and told his wife to wait in the shelter of the hedge with the two children.

'But I want to see Mrs Trigg,' she protested. 'There are lots of things we can borrow, if they went to market yesterday; not only bread, and...'

'Wait here,' Nat interrupted. 'I'll be back in a moment.'

The cows were lowing, moving restlessly in the yard, and he could see a gap in the fence where the sheep had knocked their way through, to roam unchecked in the front garden before the farm-house. No smoke came from the chimneys. He was filled with misgivings. He did not want his wife or the children to go down to the farm.

'Don't jib now,' said Nat, harshly, 'do what I say.'

She withdrew with the pram into the hedge, screening herself and the children from the wind.

He went down alone to the farm. He pushed his way through the herd of bellowing cows, which turned this way and that, distressed, their udders full. He saw the car standing by the gate, not put away in the garage. The windows of the farm-house were smashed. There were many dead gulls lying in the yard and around the house. The living birds perched on the group of trees behind the farm and on the roof of the house. They were quite still. They watched him.

Jim's body lay in the yard ... what was left of it. When the birds had finished, the cows had trampled him. His gun was beside him. The door of the house was shut and bolted, but as the windows were smashed it was easy to lift them and climb through. Trigg's body was close to the telephone. He must have been trying to get through to the exchange when the birds came for him. The receiver was hanging loose, the instrument torn from the wall. No sign of Mrs Trigg. She would be upstairs. Was it any use going up? Sickened, Nat knew what he would find.

'Thank God,' he said to himself, 'there were no children.'

He forced himself to climb the stairs, but half-way he turned and descended again. He could see her legs, protruding from the open bedroom door. Beside her were the bodies of the black-backed gulls, and an umbrella, broken.

'It's no use,' thought Nat, 'doing anything. I've only got five hours, less than that. The Triggs would understand. I must load up with what I can find.'

He tramped back to his wife and children.

'I'm going to fill up the car with stuff,' he said. 'I'll put coal in it, and paraffin for the primus. We'll take it home and return for a fresh load.'

'What about the Triggs?' asked his wife.

'They must have gone to friends,' he said.

'Shall I come and help you, then?'

'No; there's a mess down there. Cows and sheep all over the place. Wait, I'll get the car. You can sit in it.'

Clumsily he backed the car out of the yard and into the lane. His wife and the children could not see Jim's body from there.

'Stay here,' he said, 'never mind the pram. The pram can be fetched later. I'm going to load the car.'

Her eyes watched his all the time. He believed she understood, otherwise she would have suggested helping him to find the bread and groceries.

They made three journeys altogether, backwards and forwards between their cottage and the farm, before he was satisfied they had everything they needed. It was surprising, once he started thinking, how many things were necessary. Almost the most important of all was planking for the windows. He had to go round searching for timber. He wanted to renew the boards on all the windows at the cottage. Candles, paraffin, nails, tinned stuff; the list was endless. Besides all that, he milked three of the cows. The rest, poor brutes, would have to go on bellowing.

On the final journey he drove the car to the bus-stop, got out, and went to the telephone box. He waited a few minutes, jangling the receiver. No good, though. The line was dead. He climbed on to a bank and looked over the countryside, but there was no sign of life at all, nothing in the fields but the waiting, watching birds. Some of them slept – he could see the beaks tucked into the feathers.

'You'd think they'd be feeding,' he said to himself, 'not just standing in that way.'

Then he remembered. They were gorged with food. They had eaten their fill during the night. That was why they did not move this morning...

No smoke came from the chimneys of the council houses. He thought of the children who had run across the fields the night before.

'I should have known,' he thought, 'I ought to have taken them home with me.'

He lifted his face to the sky. It was colourless and grey. The bare trees on the landscape looked bent and blackened by the east wind. The cold did not affect the living birds, waiting out there in the fields.

'This is the time they ought to get them,' said Nat, 'they're a sitting target now. They must be doing this all over the country. Why don't our aircraft take off now and spray them with mustard gas? What are all our chaps doing? They must know, they must see for themselves.'

He went back to the car and got into the driver's seat.

'Go quickly past that second gate,' whispered his wife. 'The postman's lying there. I don't want Jill to see.'

He accelerated. The little Morris bumped and rattled along the lane. The children shrieked with laughter.

'Up-a-down, up-a-down,' shouted young Johnny.

It was a quarter to one by the time they reached the cottage. Only an hour to go.

'Better have cold dinner,' said Nat. 'Hot up something for yourself and the children, some of that soup. I've no time to eat now. I've got to unload all this stuff.'

He got everything inside the cottage. It could be sorted later. Give them all something to do during the long hours ahead. First he must see to the windows and the doors.

He went round the cottage methodically, testing every window, every door. He climbed on to the roof also, and fixed boards across every chimney, except the kitchen. The cold was so intense he could hardly bear it, but the job had to be done.

Now and again he would look up, searching the sky for aircraft. None came. As he worked he cursed the inefficiency of the authorities.

'It's always the same,' he muttered, 'they always let us down. Muddle, muddle, from the start. No plan, no real organization. And we don't matter, down here. That's what it is. The people up country have priority. They're using gas up there, no doubt, and all the aircraft. We've got to wait and take what comes.'

He paused, his work on the bedroom chimney finished, and looked out to sea. Something was moving out there. Something grey and white amongst the breakers.

'Good old Navy,' he said, 'they never let us down. They're coming down channel, they're turning in the bay.'

He waited, straining his eyes, watering in the wind, towards the sea. He was wrong, though. It was not ships. The Navy was not there. The gulls were rising from the sea. The massed flocks in the fields, with ruffled feathers, rose in formation from the ground, and wing to wing soared upwards to the sky.

The tide had turned again.

Nat climbed down the ladder and went inside the kitchen. The family were at dinner. It was a little after two. He bolted the door, put up the barricade, and lit the lamp.

'It's night-time,' said young Johnny.

His wife had switched on the wireless once again, but no sound came from it.

'I've been all round the dial,' she said, 'foreign stations, and that lot. I can't get anything.'

'Maybe they have the same trouble,' he said, 'maybe it's the same right through Europe.'

She poured out a plateful of the Triggs' soup, cut him a large slice of the Triggs' bread, and spread their dripping upon it.

They ate in silence. A piece of the dripping ran down young Johnny's chin and fell on to the table.

'Manners, Johnny,' said Jill, 'you should learn to wipe your mouth.'

The tapping began at the windows, at the door. The rustling, the jostling, the pushing for position on the sills. The first thud of the suicide gulls upon the step.

'Won't America do something?' said his wife. 'They've always been our allies, haven't they? Surely America will do something?'

Nat did not answer. The boards were strong against the windows, and on the chimneys too. The cottage was filled with stores, with fuel, with all they needed for the next few days. When he had finished dinner he would put the stuff away, stack it neatly, get everything shipshape, handy-like. His wife could help him, and the children too. They'd tire themselves out, between now and a quarter to nine, when the tide would ebb; then he'd tuck them down on their mattresses, see that they slept good and sound until three in the morning.

He had a new scheme for the windows, which was to fix barbed wire in front of the boards. He had brought a great roll of it from the farm. The nuisance was, he'd have to work at this in the dark, when the lull came between nine and three. Pity he had not thought of it before. Still, as long as the wife slept, and the kids, that was the main thing.

The smaller birds were at the window now. He recognized the light tap-tapping of their beaks, and the soft brush of their wings. The hawks ignored the windows. They concentrated their attack upon the door. Nat listened to the tearing sound of splintering wood, and wondered how many million years of memory were stored in those little brains, behind the stabbing beaks, the piercing eyes, now giving them this instinct to destroy mankind with all the deft precision of machines.

'I'll smoke that last fag,' he said to his wife. 'Stupid of me, it was the one thing I forgot to bring back from the farm.'

He reached for it, switched on the silent wireless. He threw the empty packet on the fire, and watched it burn.

Salman Rushdie

1947-

SALMAN RUSHDIE'S revealing story 'The Firebird's Nest' exposes the downtrodden, exploited and enslaved subjects in India, notwithstanding the fact that their potentates' powers had been abolished. It is a gruesome but liberating parable written by a brilliant author who admits that he is 'the bastard child of history'. Raised in the East and schooled in the West, his creative life has been moulded by the uneasy coalition of both poles.

Salman Rushdie was born in Bombay on 19th June 1947. He was educated in Bombay, then at Rugby School in England, and finally at King's College, Cambridge. His first novel, *Grimus*, was published in 1975. His second novel, *Midnight's Children*, published in 1981, won the Booker Prize for fiction as well as other awards. It was much praised and was eventually selected as being the Best of the Booker winners. *Shame*, his third novel, was also shortlisted for the prestigious Booker Prize. Then in 1988 *Satanic Verses*, his fourth novel, was published and immediately caused an outcry amid accusations of blasphemy against Islam. A *fatwa*, or death sentence, was issued against Rushdie and, under heavy security, he was protected by the British government.

Nevertheless, Rushdie continued to write books: *Haroun and the Sea of Stories* (1990); *Imaginary Homelands: Essays and Criticism, 1981-1991* (1992); *East, West* (1994); *The Moor's Last Sigh* (1995); *The Ground Beneath Her Feet* (1999); *Fury* (2001); *The Jaguar Smile* (1989); *Shalimar the Clown* (2005); and *The Enchantress of Florence* (2008).

The short story 'The Firebird's Nest' was first published in *The New Yorker* magazine on 23rd June 1997.

The Firebird's Nest

Now I am ready to tell how bodies are changed
Into different bodies.

– Ovid, *The Metamorphoses*
translated by Ted Hughes

IT IS A HOT PLACE, flat and sere. The rains have failed so often that now they say instead, the drought succeeded. They are plainsmen, livestock farmers, but their cattle are deserting them. The cattle, staggering, migrate south and east in search of water, and rattle as they walk. Their skulls, horned mile-posts, line the route of their vain exodus. There is water to the west, but it is salt. Soon even these marshes will have given up the ghost. There are cracks big enough to swallow a man.

An apt enough way for a farmer to die: to be eaten by his land.

Women do not die in the way. Women catch fire, and burn.

Within living memory, a thick forest stood here, Mr Maharaj tells his American bride as the limousine drives towards his palace. A rare breed of tiger lived in the forest, white as salt, wiry, small. And songbirds! A dozen dozen varieties; their very nests were built of music. Half a century ago, his father riding through the forest would hum along with their arias, could hear the tigers joining in the choruses. But now his father is dead, the tigers are extinct, and the birds have all gone, except one, which never sings a note, and, in the absence of trees, makes its nest in a secret place that has not been revealed. The firebird, he whispers, and his bride, a child of a big city, a foreigner, no virgin, laughs at such exotic melodramatics, tossing her long bright hair; which is yellow, like a flame.

There are no princes now. The government abolished them decades ago. The very idea of princes has become, in our modern country, a fiction, something from the time of feudalism, of fairytale. Their titles, their privileges have been stripped from them. They have no power over us. In this place, the prince has become plain Mr Maharaj. He is a complex man. His palace in the city has become a casino, but he heads a commission that seeks to extirpate the public corruption that is the country's bane. In his youth he was a mighty sportsman, but since his retirement he has had no time for games. He heads an ecological institute studying, and seeking remedies for, the drought; but at his country residence, at the great fortress-palace to which this limousine is taking him, cascades of precious water flow ceaselessly, for no other purpose than display. His library of ancient texts is the wonder of the province, yet he also controls the local satellite franchises, and profits from every new dish. The details of his finances, like those of his many rumoured romances, are obscure.

Here is a quarry. The limousine halts. There are men with pickaxes and women bearing earth in metal bowls upon their heads. When they see Mr Maharaj they make gestures of respect, they genuflect, they bow. The American bride, watching, intuits that she has passed into a place in which that which was abolished is the truth, and it is the government, far away in the capital, that is the fiction in which nobody believes. Here Mr Maharaj is still the prince, and she, his new princess. As though she had entered a fable, as though she were no more than words crawling along a dry page, or as though she were becoming that page itself, that surface on which her story would be written, and across which there blew a hot and merciless wind, turning her body to papyrus, her skin to parchment, her soul to paper.

It is so hot. She shivers.

It is no quarry. It is a reservoir. Farmers, driven from their land by drought, have been employed by Mr Maharaj to dig this water-hole against the day when the rains return. In this way he can give them some employment, he tells his bride, and more than employment: hope. She shakes her head, seeing that this great hollow is already full; of bitter irony. Briny, brackish, no use to man or cow.

The women in the reservoir of irony are dressed in the colours of fire. Only the foolish, blinded by language's conventions, think of fire as red, or gold. Fire is blue at its melancholy rim, green in its envious heart. It may burn white, or even, its greatest rages, black.

Yesterday, the men with pickaxes tell Mr Maharaj, a woman in a red and gold sari, a fool, ignited in the amphitheatre of the dry water-hole. The men stood along the high rim of the reservoir, watching her burn, shouldering arms in a kind of salute; recognizing, in the wisdom of their manhood, the inevitability of women's fate. The women, their women, screamed.

When the woman finished burning there was nothing there. Not a scrap of flesh, not a bone. She burned as paper burns, flying up to the sky and being blown into nothing by the wind.

The combustibility of women is a source of resigned wonder to the men hereabouts. They just burn too easily, what's to be done about it? Turn your back and they're alight. Perhaps it is a difference between the sexes, the men say. Men are earth, solid, enduring, but the ladies are capricious, unstable, they are not long for this world, they go off in a puff of smoke without leaving so much as a note of explanation. And in this heat, if they should spend too long in the sun! We tell them to stay indoors, not to expose themselves to danger, but you know how women are. It is their fate, their nature.

Even the demure ones have fiery hearts; perhaps the demure ones most of all, Mr Maharaj murmurs to his wife in the limousine. She is a woman of modern outlook and does not like it, she tells him, when he speaks this way, herding her sex into these crude corrals, these easy generalisations, even in jest. He inclines his head in amused apology. A firebrand, he says. I see I must mend my ways.

See that you do, she commands, and nestles comfortably under his arm. His grey beard brushes her brow.

Gossip burns ahead of her. She is rich, as rich as the old, obese Nizam of ———, who was weighed in jewels on his birthdays and so was able to increase taxes simply by putting on weight. His subjects would quake as they saw his banquets, his mighty halvas, his towering jellies, his kulfi Himalayas, for they knew that the endless avalanche of delicacies sliding down the Nizam's gullet meant that the food on their own tables would be sparse and plain, as he wept with exhausted repletion so their children would weep with hunger, his gluttony would be their famine. Yes, filthy rich, the gossip sizzles, her American father claims descent from the deposed royal family of an Eastern European state, and each year he flies the elite employees of his commercial empire by private aircraft to his lost kingdom, where by the banks of the River of Time itself he stages a four-day golf tournament, and then, laughing, contemptuous, godlike, fires the champion, destroys his life for the hubris of aspiring to glory, abandons him by the shores of Time's River, into whose tumultuous, deadly waters the champion finally dives, and is lost, like hope, like a ball.

She is rich; she is a fertile land; she will bring sons, and rain. No, she is poor, the gossip flashes, her father hanged himself when she was born, her mother was a whore, she also is a creature of wildernesses and rocky ground, the drought is in her body, like a curse, she is barren, and has come in the hope of stealing brown babies from their homes and nursing them from bottles, since her own breasts are dry.

Mr Maharaj has searched the world for its treasures and brought back a magic jewel whose light will change their lives. Mr Maharaj has fallen into iniquity and brought Despair into his palace, has succumbed to yellow-haired doom.

So she is becoming a story the people tell, and argue over. Travelling towards the palace, she too is aware, of entering a story, a group of stories about women such as herself, fair and yellow, and the dark men they loved. She was warned by friends at home, in her tall city. Do not go with him, they cautioned her. If you sleep with him, he will not respect you. He does not think of women like you as wives. Your otherness excites him, your freedom. He will break your heart.

Though he calls her his bride, she is not his wife. So far, she feels no fear.

A ruined gateway stands in the wilderness, an entrance to nowhere. A single tree, the last of all the local trees to fall, lies rotting beside it, the exposed roots grabbing at air like a dead giant's hand. A wedding party passes, and the limousine slows. She sees that the turbaned groom, on his way to meet his wife, is not young and eager, but wisp-haired, old and parched; she imagines a tale of undying love, long denied by circumstance, overcoming adversity at last. Somewhere an elderly sweetheart awaits her wizened amour. They have loved each other always, she imagines, and now near their stories' conclusion they have found this happy ending. By accident she speaks these words aloud. Mr Maharaj smiles, and shakes his head. The bridegroom's bride is young, a virgin from a distant village.

Why would a pretty young girl wish to marry an old fool? Mr Maharaj shrugs. The old fellow will have settled for a small dowry, he replies, and if one has many daughters such factors have much weight. As for the oldster, he adds, in a long life there may be more than a single dowry. These things add up.

Flutes and horns blow raucous music in her direction. A drum crumps like cannon-fire. Transsexual dancers heckle her through the window. Ohé, America, they screech, arré, howdy-podner, say what? Okay, you take care now, I'm-a-yankee-doodle-dandy! Ooh, baby, wah-wah, maximum cool. Miss America, shake that thing! She feels a sudden panic. Drive faster, she cries, and the driver accelerates. Dust explodes around the wedding party, hiding it from view. Mr Maharaj is solicitude personified, but she is angry with herself. Excuse me, she mutters. It's nothing. The heat.

('America'. Once upon a time in 'America', they had shared an Indian lunch three hundred feet above street-level, at a table with a view of the vernal lushness of the park, feasting their eyes upon an opulence of vegetation which now, as she remembers it in this desiccated landscape, feels obscene. My country is just like yours, he'd said, flirting. Big, turbulent and full of gods. We speak our kind of bad English and you speak yours. And before you became Romans, when you were just colonials, our masters were the same. You defeated them before we did. So now you have more money than we do. Otherwise, we're the same. On your street corners the same bustle of differences, the same litter, the same everything-at-onceness. She guessed immediately what he was telling her: that he came from a place unlike anything she had ever experienced, whose languages she would struggle to master, whose codes she might never break and whose immensity and mystery would provoke and fulfil her greatest passion and her deepest need.

Because she was an American, he spoke to her of money. The old protectionist legislation, the outdated socialism that had hobbled the economy for so long, had been repealed and there were fortunes to be made if you had the ideas. Even a prince had to be on the ball, one step ahead of the game. He was bursting with projects, and she had a reputation in financial circles as a person who could bring together capital and ideas, who could conjure up, for her favoured projects, the monetary nourishment they required.

A 'rainmaker'.

She took him to the opera, was aroused, as always, by the power of great matters sung of in words she could not understand, whose meaning had to be inferred from the performers' deeds. Then she took him home and seduced him. It was her city, her stage, and she was confident, and young. As they began to make love, she guessed that she was about to leave behind everything she knew, all the roots of her self. Her lovemaking became ferocious, as if his body were a locked gateway to the unknown, and she must batter it down.

Not everything will be wonderful, he warned her. There is a terrible drought.

His palace, unfortunately, is abominable. It crumbles, stinks. In her room, the curtains are tattered, the bed precarious, the pictures on the wall pornographic representations of arabesque couplings at some petty princeling's court. No way of knowing if these are her husband's ancestors or a job-lot purchased from a persuasive pedlar. Loud music plays in ill-lit corridors, but she cannot find its source. Shadows scurry from her sight. He installs her, vanishes, without an explanation. She is left to make herself at home.

That night, she sleeps alone. A ceiling fan stirs the hot, syrupy air. It simmers, like a soup. She cannot stop thinking of 'home': its nocturnal sirens, its cooling machinery. Its reification of the real. Amid that surplus of structures, of content, it is not easy for the phantasmagoric to gain the upper hand. Our entertainment is full of monsters, of the fabulous, because outside the darkened cinemas, beyond the pages of the books, away from the gothic decibels of the music, the quotidian is inescapable, omnipotent. We dream of other dimensions, of paranoid subtexts, of underworlds, because when we awake the actual holds us in its great thingy grasp and we cannot see beyond the material, the event horizon. Whereas here, caught in the empty bubbling of dry air, afraid of roaches, all your frontiers may crumble; are crumbling. The possibility of the terrible is renewed.

She has never found it easy to weep, but her body convulses. She cries dry tears, and sleeps. When she awakes there is the sound of a drum, and dancers.

✶

In a courtyard, the women and girls are gathered, young and old. The drummer beats out a rhythm and the ladies respond in unison. Their knees bent outward, their splay-fingered hands semaphoring at the ends of peremptory arms, their necks making impossible, lateral shifts, eyes ablaze, they advance across cool stone like a syncopated army. (It is still early, and the courtyard is in shadow; the sun has not yet lent the stone its fire.) At the dancers' head, tallest of them all, fiercely erect, showing them how, is Maharaj's sister, over sixty years old, but still the greatest dancer in the state, Miss Maharaj has seen the newcomer, but makes no acknowledgement. She is mistress of the dance. Movement is all.

When it's finished, they face each other, Mr Maharaj's women: the sister, the American.

What are you doing?

A dance against the firebird. A propitiatory dance, to ward it off.

The firebird. (She thinks of Stravinsky, of Lincoln Center.)

Miss Maharaj inclines her head. The bird which never sings, she says. Whose nest is secret; whose malevolent wings brush women's bodies, and we burn.

But surely there is no such bird. It's just an old wives' tale.

Here there are no old wives' tales. Alas, there are no old wives.

Enter Mr Maharaj! Turbaned, with an embroidered cloth flung about his broad shoulders, how handsome, how manly, how winsomely apologetic!

She finds herself behaving petulantly, like a woman from another age. He woos and cajoles. He went to prepare her welcome. He hopes she will approve.

What is it?

Wait and see.

In the semi-desert beyond his stinking palace, Mr Maharaj has prepared an extravaganza. By moonlight, beneath hot stars, on great carpets from Isfahan and Shiraz, a gathering of dignitaries and nobles welcomes her, the finest musicians play their mournful, haunting flutes, their ecstatic strings, and sing the most ancient and freshest love-songs ever heard; the most succulent delicacies of the region are offered for her delight. She is already famous in the neighbourhood, a great celebrity. I invited your husband to visit us, the governor of an adjacent state guffaws, but I told him, if you don't bring your beautiful lady, don't bother to show up. A neighbouring ex-prince offers to show her the art treasures locked in his palace vaults. I take them out for nobody, he says, except Mrs Onassis, of course. For you, I will spread them in my garden, as I did for Jackie O.

While the moonlight lasts, there are camel-races and horse-races, dancing and song. Fireworks burst over their heads. She leans against Mr Maharaj, his absence long forgiven, and whispers, you have made a magic kingdom for me, or (she teases him) is this how you relax every night?

She feels him stiffen, smells the bitterness leaking from his words. It is you who have made this happen, he replies. In this ruined place you have conjured this illusion. The camels, the horses, even the food has been brought from far away. We impoverish ourselves to make you happy. How can you imagine that we are able to live like this? We protect the last fragments of what we had, and now, to please you, we plunge deeper into debt. We dream only of survival; this Arabian night is an American dream.

I asked for nothing, she said. This conspicuous consumption is not my fault. Your accusation, your diatribe, is offensive.

He has had too much to drink, and it has made him truthful. It is our obeisance, he tells us, at the feet of power. Rainmaker, bring us rain.

Money, you mean.

What else? Is there anything else?

I thought there was love, she says.

The full moon has never looked more beautiful. No music has ever sounded lovelier. No night has ever felt so cruel. She says: I have something to tell you.

She is pregnant. She dreams of burning bridges, of burning boats. She dreams of a movie she has always loved, in which a man returns to his ancestral village, and somehow slips through time, to the time of his father's youth. When he tries to flee the village, and returns to the railway station, the tracks have disappeared. There is no way home. This is where the film ends.

When she awakes from her dream, in her sweltering room, the sheets are soaked and there is a woman sitting at her bedside. She gathers a wet sheet around her nakedness. Miss Maharaj smiles, shrugs. You have a strong body, she says. Younger, but in other ways not so unlike mine.

I would have left him. Now I just don't know.

Miss Maharaj shakes her head. In the village they say it will be a boy, she explains, and then the drought will break. Just superstition. But he can't let you leave. And afterwards, if you go, he'll keep the child.

We'll see about that! she blasts. When she is agitated her tones become nasal, unattractive even to herself. In her mind's eye the story is closing around her, the story in which she is trapped, and in which she must, if she can, find the path of action: preferably of right action, but if not, then of wrong. What cannot be tolerated is inertia. She will not fall into some tame and heat-dazed swoon. Romance has led her into errors enough. Now she will use her head.

Slowly, as the weeks unfold, she begins to see. He does not own the casino in his palace in the city, has signed a foolish contract, letting it to a consortium of alarming men. The rent they pay him is absurd, and it is stipulated in the small print that on certain high days each year he must hang around the gaming-tables, grinning ingratiatingly at the guests, lending a tone. The satellite-dish franchises are more lucrative, but this greedy old wreck of a country residence needs to eat off far richer platters if it's to be properly fed.

This rural palace is ageless: perhaps six hundred years. Most of it lacks electricity, windows, furniture. Cold in the cold season, hot in the heat, and if the rains should come, many of its staterooms would flood. All they have here is water, their inexhaustible palace spring. At the back of the palace, past the ruined zones where the bats hold sway, she picks her way through accumulated guano and sees a line form before dawn. The villagers, rendered indigent by the drought, come under cover of darkness, hiding their humiliation, filling their supplicant pitchers. Behind the line of the thirsty there stands, like a haunting, the high black shadow of a crenellated wall. A village woman with a few unaccountable words of English explains that this charred fortress was, in former days, the larger part of the prince's residence. Great treasures were lost when it burned; also, lives.

When did this happen?

In before time.

She begins to understand his bitterness. Another princess, Miss Maharaj tells her, a dowager even more destitute than we, recently ended her life by drinking fire. She crushed her heirloom diamonds in a cup and gulped them down.

So Mr Maharaj, visiting America, had turned himself into an illusion of sophistication and innovation, had won her with a desperate performance. He has learned to talk like a modern man but in truth is helpless in the face of the present. The drought, his unworldliness, the decision of history to turn away her face, these things are his undoing. In Greece, the athlete who won the Olympic race became a person of high rank in his home state. Mr Maharaj, however, rots, as does his house. Her own room begins to look like luxury's acme. Glass in the windows, the slow-turning electric fan. A telephone with, sometimes, a dialling tone. A socket for her laptop's power line, the intermittent possibility of forging a modern link with that other planet, her earlier life.

He has not taken her to his own room because he is ashamed of it.

Sensing the life growing inside her, she wants to forgive its father; to help him out of the past, into that flowing, meta-morphic present which has been her real life. She will do what she can do. She is 'America', and brings the rain.

Again and again she awakes, sweating, naked, with Miss Maharaj murmuring at her side. Yes, a fine body, it could have been a dancer's. It will burn well.

Don't touch me! (She is alarmed.)

All brides in these parts are brought from far afield. And once the men have spent their dowries, then the firebird comes.

Don't threaten me! (Perplexed.)

Do you know how many brides he has had?

Terrified, raging, bewildered, she confronts him. Is it true? Is that why your sister has never married, why she gathers under her roof, to protect them, all the spinsters of the village, young and old? That interminable dance class of lifetime virgins, too frightened to take a husband?

Is it true you burn your brides?

Ah, my mad sister has been whispering to you, he laughs. She came to your room at night, she caressed your body, she spoke of water and fire, of women's beauty and the secret, lethal nature of men. She told you about the magic bird, I suppose. The bird of death.

No, she remembers, carefully. The one who first named the firebird was you.

Mr Maharaj in a fury brings her to his sister's dance class. Seeing him, the dancers stumble, their bell-braceleted feet lose the rhythm and come jangling to a halt. Why are you here, he asks them, raging. Tell my bride why you have come. Are you refugees or students? Sir, students. Are you here because you are afraid? Oh, please, sir, we are not afraid. His inquisition is relentless, bellowing, and all the while his eyes never leave his sister's. Miss Maharaj stands tall and silent.

The last question is for her. How many brides have I had? How many do you say? They are locked in each other's power, brother and sister, each other's eternal prisoners, outside history, beyond time. Miss Maharaj is the first to drop her eyes. She is the first, she says.

It's over. He turns to face his bride, and spreads his arms. You heard it with your own ears. Let's have no more of fables.

The heat is maddening. Skeletal bullocks die on the brown lawn. Some days, there are mustard-yellow clouds filling the sky, hanging over the evaporating marshes to the west. Even this hideous yellow rain would be welcome, but it does not fall.

Everyone has bad breath. All exhale serpents, dead cats, insects, fogs. Everyone's perspiration is thick, and stinks.

In spite of all her resolutions, the heat hypnotises her. This child grows. Miss Maharaj's dancers become careless about closing doors and windows. They are to be glimpsed, here and there, painting one another's bodies in hot colours and wild designs, making love, sleeping with limbs entwined. Mr Maharaj does not come to her, will not, while she is 'carrying'. But each night, Miss Maharaj comes. Since her brother's descent upon her dance class, Miss Maharaj has barely spoken. At night she asks only to sit at the bedside, sometimes, almost primly, to touch. This, Mr Maharaj's American bride allows.

Her health fails. She begins to sweat, to shiver from a fever. Her shit is like thin mud. Only the palace spring saves her from dehydration and swift death. Miss Maharaj nurses her, brings her salt. The only physician hereabouts is an old fellow, out of touch, useless. Both women know the baby is at risk.

During these long, sick nights, quietly, absently, the sexa-genarian dancer talks.

Something frightful has happened here. Some irreversible transformation. Without our noticing its beginnings, so that we did not resist until it was too late, until the new way of things was fixed, there has occurred a terrible, terminal rupture between our men and women. When men say they fear the absence of rain, when women say we fear the presence of fire, this is what we mean. Something has been unleashed in us. It's too late to tame it now.

Once upon a time there was a great prince here. The last prince, one could say. Everything about him was gigantic, mythological. The most handsome prince in the world, he married the most beautiful bride, a legendary dancer and temptress, and they had two children, a girl and a boy. As he aged, his strength ebbed, his eye dimmed, but she, the dancer, refused to fade. At the age of fifty she had the look of a young woman of twenty-one. As the prince's force faded, as that glamour which had been the heart of his power ceased to work its magic, so his jealousy increased...

(Miss Maharaj shrugged, moved quickly to the story's end.)

The fortress burned. They both died. He had suspected his wife of taking lovers but there had been none. The children, who had been left in the care of servants, lived. The daughter became a dancer and the son, a sportsman, and so on. And the villagers said that the old prince, consumed by rage, had been transformed into a giant bird, a bird composed entirely of flames, and that was the bird that burned the princess, and returns, these days, to turn other women to ashes at their husbands' cruel command.

And you, asks the ill woman on the bed. What do you say?

Do not condescend to us in your heart, Miss Maharaj replies. Do not mistake the abnormal for the untrue. We are caught in metaphors. They transfigure us, and reveal the meaning of our lives.

The illness recedes and the baby seems also to be well. The return of health is like a curtain being lifted. She is thinking like herself again. She will keep the child, but will no longer be trapped in this place of fantasies with a man she finds she does not know. She will go to the city, fly back to America, and after the child is born, what will be, will be. A quick divorce, of course. She has no desire to prevent the father from seeing his child. Extremely free access, including trips East, will be granted. She wants that, wants the child to know both cultures. Enough! Time to behave like an adult. She may even continue to advise Mr Maharaj on his financial needs. Why not? It's her job. She tells Miss Maharaj her decision, and the old dancer winces, as if from a blow.

In the dead of night, the American is awakened by a hubbub in the palace, in its corridors and courtyard. She dresses, goes outside. A scratch armada of motor vehicles has assembled: a rusty bus, several motor-scooters, a newish Japanese people carrier, an open truck, a Jeep in camouflage. Miss Maharaj's women are piling into the vehicles, angry, singing. They have taken weapons, the domestic weapons that came to hand, sticks, garden implements, kitchen knives. At their head, revving the Jeep, shouting impatiently at her troops, is Miss Maharaj.

What's going on?

None of your business. You don't believe in fairies. You're going home.

I'm coming with you.

Miss Maharaj treats the Jeep roughly, driving it at speed over broken ground, without lights. The motley convoy jolts along behind. They drive by the light of a molten full moon.

Ahead of them stands a ruined stone arch, an entrance to nothing, beside a fallen tree. The armada halts, turns on its lights. The dance class pours through the archway, as if it were the only possible entrance to the open waste ground beyond, as if it were the portal to another world. When she, the American, does likewise, she has that feeling again: of passing through an invisible membrane, a looking glass, into another kind of truth; into fiction.

A tableau, illuminated by the lights of motor vehicles. Remember the old bridegroom, on his way to meet his young, imported bride? Here he is again, guilty, murderous, and his young wife, uncomprehending, at his side.

In the background, silhouetted, are the figures of male villagers. Facing the unhappy couple is Mr Maharaj.

The women burst shrieking upon the charmless scene, then come raggedly to a halt, intimidated by Mr Maharaj's presence. The sister faces the brother. Somebody has left their lights flashing. The siblings' faces glow white, yellow, red in the headlights. They speak in a language the American cannot understand, it is an opera without overtitles, she must infer what they are saying from their actions, from their thoughts made deeds, and so, as clearly as if she comprehended every syllable, she hears Miss Maharaj command her brother, what started between our parents stops now, and his response, a response that has no meaning in the world beyond the ruined archway, which he speaks as his body turns to fire, as the wings burst out of him, as his eyes blaze; his words hang in the air as the firebird's breath scorches Miss Maharaj, burns her to a cinder and then turns upon the dotard's shrieking bride.

I am the firebird's nest. Something loosens within the American as she sees Miss Maharaj burn, some shackle is broken, some limit of possibility passed. Unleashed, she crashes upon Mr Maharaj like a wave, and the angry dancers pour behind her, seething, irresistible. They feel the frontiers of their bodies burst and the waters pour out, the immense crushing weight of their rain, drowning the firebird and its nest, flowing over the drought-hardened land that no longer knows how to absorb the flood which bears away the old dotard and his murderous fellows, cleansing the region of its horrors, of its archaic tragedies, of its men.

The flood waters ebb, like anger. The women become themselves again, and the universe too resumes its familiar shape. The women huddle patiently under the old stone arch, listening for helicopters, waiting to be rescued from the deluge of themselves, freed from fear. As for the American, her own shape will continue to change. Mr Maharaj's child will be born, not here but in her own country, to which she will soon return. Increasing, she caresses her swelling womb. The new life growing within her will be both fire and rain.

November, 1998

Christopher Ondaatje

1933-

CHRISTOPHER ONDAATJE's short story 'The Devil Bird' was inspired while he was researching his auto-biographical memoir *The Man-Eater of Punanai* (1992) in the south-east jungles of Sri Lanka. It is a story fraught with superstition and fear.

Christopher Ondaatje was born in Kandy, Ceylon on 22nd February 1933, educated in England, and emigrated to Canada in 1956. He has worked at several magazines and newspapers and in 1967 founded Pagurian Press, which eventually became the enormously successful Pagurian Corporation. In 1988 he sold all his business interests and returned to the literary world.

He is the author of ten books including the best-selling Burton biographies *Sindh Revisited* (1996) and *Journey to the Source of the Nile* (1998); and more recently *Hemingway in Africa* (2003), *Woolf in Ceylon* (2005), *The Power of Paper* (2006) and *The Glenthorne Cat* (2008). He was a member of Canada's 1964 Olympic bobsled team, is a fellow of both the Royal Geographical Society and the Royal Society of Literature and was, until 2009, a trustee of the National Portrait Gallery. He lives in London, England and was knighted by the Queen in 2003.

The Devil Bird

O F COURSE I had heard about the notorious devil bird. I first heard about it on Kuttapitiya – the tea estate in Ceylon where my father worked and where we children grew up. But that was a very long time ago in the 1940s, before I was sent to England 'to get a decent education'. Ours was a wild, carefree existence, and we were happy. I particularly remember 1946 when my father took me on a trip around the Island. It was probably the highlight of my life up until then. I was twelve, and it was certainly the last thing we did alone together. Our final journey took us by car and driver from the estate, first down to the Yala Game Reserve on the southeast coast, and then north to the ancient cities of Sigiriya, Anuradhapura, and Polonnaruwa. More than any other member of the family, my father and I shared a love of the outdoors and of wildlife; it was a great bond that he had encouraged between us on our walks around the estate or on holidays.

'Christopher, do you want to come?' he used to yell as he set off on his inspections, and I accompanied him, partly because I loved him so much and partly because he would be angry if I didn't go. As he walked, he taught me about history, about nature, about confidence, and he always encouraged me in any interest I had, whether it was in birds or athletics or boating. It was then that he first told me about the devil bird. It is rarely seen, and there is still a debate about what it is. Suggestions include a brown wood owl and a crested honey buzzard, but the best evidence, amassed in 1968 by Dr. R.L. Spittel, suggests it is either the crested hawk eagle or the forest eagle owl. Whatever its identity, there is a local super-stition that the devil bird is an omen of death.

According to the ancient legend, once there was a jealous hus-band who suspected his wife of infidelity. During her absence he murdered their child and made a curry from the corpse. He served it to his wife, who ate it until she found the baby's finger on her plate. Mad with grief and disgust, she fled into the jungle and killed herself, but the Gods transformed her into a bird, the devil bird, which still horrifies the world with the woman's hysterical screams.

The cry of the devil bird has also been compared to the sound of a baby being strangled, a boy being tortured, and a lost child whose wailings break off into a pitiful choking sob. Dr. Spittel found a variation of the myth in the folklore of the Veddahs, the Island's earliest inhabitants. A Veddah and his son Koa were out hunting for three days without success. They were both very hungry. The father told his son to kindle a fire and, when it was aflame, thrust his son Koa into it, roasted him, and ate some of the flesh. He took part of it to his wife, who cooked it and was sharing it out when she suddenly became aware that it was her son's flesh. Digging the handle of the spoon into her head, she screamed, 'Koa!', fled into the forest and died. And now, as the crested ulama, she makes the midnight jungle echo with that wail.

Even stranger are the tragic tales told by a man named Shelley Crozier, who went hunting on three occasions in the 1920s with three different friends to the same waterhole in the remote Eastern Province. Each time he heard the devil bird cry under a full moon. The first time was with his friend Phillip, like Crozier a special apprentice with the Railway.

'Here was a whitish brown bird with a hooked beak and about the size of a hawk, craning its neck to get a better look at us,' Crozier reported. 'When exactly opposite my friend, it stretched its neck forward, puffed its neck feathers out and then shattered the silence with its deadly scream. Screaming and shaking its head up and down, as though he was abusing my friend, he shut up and was about to fly off when I shot it a bare foot away from the point of my gun. My friend was sweating from every pore of his body, and by the light of the moon he looked as pale as death.'

'I am not long for this world,' Phillip prophesied. Then at dawn, seeing the dead bird, he shouted, 'For God's sake take me from here.' Five days later Phillip was struck by a bus. 'The curse of the devil bird,' he said to Crozier in the hospital, and died.

The next year, Crozier visited the same place with another friend. They heard the horrible scream and the bird flew out of the night and dropped a chameleon onto his friend's lap. He laughed it off, but four days later he became ill and was sent to hospital. 'Devil bird,' he whispered to Crozier, and died.

The following year, in exactly the same place, Crozier was with yet another friend, Noël. Noël, too, had been warned, but insisted on making the trip. 'Devil or angel, I stay,' Noël said bravely at first. But as the darkness came, his courage departed. 'Let's can this damn shoot and get out of here, even if we have to get lost!' he said. But they didn't go, nor did they sleep. Then the scream. 'I am bloody sorry I came,' Noël said. An hour later another scream, and the bird flew low over Noël's head. Two weeks later he was dead.

Rather belatedly, Crozier decided not to tempt fate any further, stating: 'I vowed that I would never again take a friend to that place as long as I lived.'

All these stories of the devil bird, and the warnings my father had given me when I was a child, swirled around in my head when I returned to Sri Lanka in 1991, after forty years, to research *The Man-Eater of Punanai* – a bitter-sweet memoir of my early life on the island, and an attempt to grapple with the ghost of my father. I was also going to re-tell the story of the Punanai leopard that had killed and devoured at least twenty human beings in the region of Punanai, keeping the tiny village in terror. Childers Jayawardena, Lakshman Senatilleke and I, therefore, intent on retracing the last trip I had made with my father, headed first south to Yala, then north to the ruined cities, and eventually to Punanai to learn more about the man eater. It was an unsettling time in Sri Lanka.

Throughout the fall and winter of 1989, as I was getting ready to return, the newspapers were full of stories about Sri Lanka's civil war. Government troops were clashing with rebels, bombs were exploding in markets and buses, and innocent people were getting killed in the process. The country was a virtual powder keg. We knew we might get caught in the cross-fire between several warring factions, but our determination to succeed in our eight-week research safari overrode all other considerations – even the threat of danger. From Colombo we headed for Galle, then to Hambantota and the flat, dry, yellowy-brown scrubland that I love so much; and then, via Tissamaharama, to the arid and sandy terrain that makes up the four hundred square mile Yale Game Sanctuary. It was to be our home for the first four weeks.

We searched for leopards, of course, spending the first few days in the Talgasmankada bungalow – a small building, just a couple of rooms and an L-shaped verandah, on the bank of the Menik river. Its name means the crossing where the thal trees are. The bungalow was almost bare of furnishings and had no electricity and only a little water, but it was wonderfully shaded by huge deciduous trees. Almost immediately we felt free. The only telephone connection was from Tissamaharama forty miles away. We had to go out every few days for fresh food. Other than that, news of fighting in the area or reports of murders reached us only by word of mouth. Eventually we began to clear our minds, to the point that all we really cared about was if we had a pair of dry shoes, a hat against the sun, and a dose of mosquito repellent.

We slept out on the verandah. The rooms were too hot, so a row of cots was placed along the gallery facing the river. I noticed that Lucky and Childers chose cots in the centre, leaving me with the first bed a wild animal would come to on its nocturnal prowl. But we all got used to our positions, including the park trackers. The days were long, tracking leopards and interviewing people. We learned to be patient, and looked forward to the magical night and the smell of the kerosene lamps. We slept well. The breeze was cool and there were no mosquitoes. From time to time I was awakened by a sound and shone my flashlight into the eerie blackness, catching the inquisitive eyes of deer and hares and squirrels. We got used to occasional angry cries of the peacocks too, and sometimes slept through the rasping, sawing sound of a leopard from across the river.

And then on the fourth night we slept again on the verandah, but with less success. There were louder and more disturbing jungle noises, and neither Childers nor Lucky seemed able to settle down. Deep in the night a shot rang out. Again, it came from the other side of the river, perhaps a mile away. Terrorists? I knew the others were awake, but nobody moved or said anything. The sharp crack of a rifle set off a frenzied chorus of shrieks, led by the peacocks and a couple of langurs, and amidst them came a blood-curdling scream. I froze. No one made a sound. It really did sound like a child being strangled. I lay tense and wide awake until the commotion quietened down and I was able to drop off to sleep.

The morning brought a change of plan that seemed another ill omen. Originally we were intending to spend five days in Talgasmankada, go off to another part of the park for a while, then return for five more days. Now, we were instructed to go immediately to the Patanangala bungalow on the coast. Childers, a former game warden, explained that this was to allow him to pursue his research about turtles, but I suspected that he and Lucky had decided that it would be safer to move away from the bungalow. The Talgasmankada bungalow had already been burned to the ground a couple of years before, and it was on the main escape route for terrorists trying to flee north into the interior from the coast. The fighting was getting closer. I wanted to forget about devil birds and terrorists as I was much more interested in looking for leopards. It wasn't a particularly good atmosphere and I wasn't quite sure why. Wanniarachchi, one of the trackers, was particularly quiet and seemed very edgy. We packed quickly before having breakfast, and had piled into the jeeps heading away from Talgasmankada shortly after sunrise. I was in one jeep with Lucky, Wanniarachchi and Raja – our driver. Childers followed in the other jeep with the other tracker, driver and the bags. We made our way on the jungle track to Patanangala. The jungle seemed very still.

Almost in silence, our two jeeps cut across, first down the Gona Lahaba road, along the main Yala road, and were just about to turn left down the Patanangala road to the sea when Wanniarachchi, silent until now, burst into a stream of agitated Sinhalese, talking to Lucky mainly, and to Raja, who stopped the jeep very suddenly, letting Childers pass us and then turn towards the Patanangala bungalow. Lucky too now seemed agitated, looking from Wanniarachchi to Raja and back again. No one said anything for a while and then Lucky looked to me and said, 'Chris, we must go to Kataragama immediately. This is important. Wanniarachchi's daughter has a young baby girl and he is worried that she may be sick. I think it's the devil bird. It's the first time he's ever heard it.' Then silence. 'Shall I drop you off at the bungalow and then go with Wanniarachchi to Kataragama and come back a bit later?' Lucky asked.

'No,' I said, 'we must all go. Let's quickly go to the bungalow, tell Childers, and then proceed to Kataragama now. If the baby is ill we must do what we can right away.'

It took us a few minutes to get to the Patanangala bungalow, where we explained what the problem was, and turned around and drove back to the Talgasmankada road, to the Katagamuwa entrance to the park, and then the six miles to Kataragama, eleven miles northeast of Tissamaharama. The path that has brought pilgrims of all faiths through the jungle for hundreds of years was now a red gravel road, but thousands still walk the route through 'God's country,' chanting, 'Haro Hara.' We were silent, serious, intent. The last stretch took us almost into the Kataragama town before Wanniarachchi directed Raja to turn left down Vallimath-agama Road to a humble thatched wattle and daub hut at the end of the road. Both Wanniarachchi and Lucky got out immediately. I stayed in the jeep with Raja. Wanniarachchi didn't knock, he simply opened the door. But his daughter, quite unconcerned, was already there to greet him. However, after an intense conversation in Sinhalese, a horrific expression appeared on the daughter's face, after which both the daughter and Wanniarachchi disappeared into the house, leaving the door open. I could see them hurrying to a corridor leading to a far corner of the dwelling. Lucky stayed outside the house, smoking and fidgeting nervously. We said nothing, fearing the worst.

But after a few minutes, perhaps eight or nine, they reappeared, this time with the two-year-old daughter in her mother's arms. They both still had a terrified look on their faces. Wanniarachchi's granddaughter seemed to be perfectly all right but there continued a serious dialogue between father and daughter for some time before Lucky and the tracker climbed back in the jeep. Nothing was said, and I asked no questions. Then, just as we turned off the highway into the park, Lucky turned to me and said, 'You know, Chris, I am not a particularly superstitious man, and I think I have heard the devil bird a few times in my life. But Wanniarachchi has not, and last night must have triggered something in his mind. He was very nervous, and convinced that something terrible had happened to his granddaughter. That's why he insisted on going to Kataragama right away. He wouldn't have asked normally because he knows how important this work you are doing is to you, but he was certain that a curse had been thrown on his family, and particularly on his daughter. The amazing thing is he may have been right, and we may have only got there just in time. The little girl was in her room asleep, but when Wanniarachchi and his daughter went to her they found her head stuck between the bars of her cot. Anything might have happened. They had an awful time getting the little girl's head free and back through the bars. Wanniarachchi's daughter was in a terrible state. Anyway, it's a lucky thing we came right away. I don't know about this devil bird but there are so many stories and so many warnings that it is no wonder people are terrified when they hear the bird's scream.'

We drove back to our Park bungalow in silence.

Edgar Allan Poe

1809-1849

'THE RAVEN' is by far the best known of Edgar Allan Poe's poems. It features a young man grieving over the loss of his young love, Lenore, and a mysterious dark foreboding bird, a raven, who speaks but a single word to the grief-stricken young man. It has over time become the best known and most frequently parodied American poem ever written.

Edgar Allan Poe was born on 19th January 1809 to Elizabeth Arnold Hopkins and David Poe, Jr., who were members of a repertory company in Boston, Massachusetts. He was only three years old when he was orphaned and placed in the care of Fanny and John Allan, who never legally adopted him. He was given an excellent schooling, including acceptance at the University of Virginia. However, he fell out with his surrogate father over his chronic gambling habits, who stripped him of any further financial support. He left home and enlisted in the army. He published several collections of poems, in 1827, 1829 and 1831, before accepting an editorial post at *The Southern Literary Messenger* in Richmond, Virginia. It was to be the first of many such positions. The publication of 'The Raven' in 1845 achieved his highest measure of critical acclaim, but his increasingly popular recognition was marked with sickness and economic turmoil. His young wife died of tuberculosis in 1847, after which he became increasingly addicted to alcohol. He died in Baltimore on 7th October 1849. He was only forty years old.

The Raven

Once upon a midnight dreary, while I pondered, weak and
  weary,
Over many a quaint and curious volume of forgotten lore –
While I nodded, nearly napping, suddenly there came a tapping,
As of someone gently rapping, rapping at my chamber door.
' 'T is some visitor,' I muttered, 'tapping at my chamber door –
  Only this and nothing more.'

Ah, distinctly I remember it was in the bleak December;
And each separate dying ember wrought its ghost upon the
  floor.
Eagerly I wished the morrow; – vainly I had sought to borrow
From my books surcease of sorrow – sorrow for the lost Lenore,
For the rare and radiant maiden whom the angels name
  Lenore –
  Nameless here for evermore.

And the silken, sad, uncertain rustling of each purple curtain
Thrilled me – filled me with fantastic terrors never felt before;
So that now, to still the beating of my heart, I stood repeating
' 'T is some visitor entreating entrance at my chamber door –
Some late visitor entreating entrance at my chamber door; –
  This it is and nothing more.'

Presently my soul grew stronger; hesitating then no longer,
'Sir,' said I, 'or Madam, truly your forgiveness I implore;

But the fact is I was napping, and so gently you came rapping,
And so faintly you came tapping, tapping at my chamber door,
That I scarce was sure I heard you' – here I opened wide the
    door; –
            Darkness there and nothing more.

Deep into that darkness peering, long I stood there wondering,
    fearing,
Doubting, dreaming dreams no mortal ever dared to dream
    before;
But the silence was unbroken, and the stillness gave no token,
And the only word there spoken was the whispered word,
    'Lenore!'
This I whispered, and an echo murmured back the word
    'Lenore!'
            Merely this and nothing more.

Back into the chamber turning, all my soul within me
    burning,
Soon again I heard a tapping somewhat louder than before.
'Surely,' said I, 'surely that is something at my window lattice;
Let me see, then, what thereat is, and this mystery explore –
Let my heart be still a moment and this mystery explore;
            'T is the wind and nothing more!'

Open here I flung the shutter, when, with many a flirt and
    flutter,
In there stepped a stately Raven of the saintly days of yore.
Not the least obeisance made he; not a minute stopped or stayed
    he;
But, with mien of lord or lady, perched above my chamber
    door –
Perched upon a bust of Pallas just above my chamber door –
            Perched, and sat, and nothing more.

Then this ebony bird beguiling my sad fancy into smiling,
By the grave and stern decorum of the countenance it wore,
'Though thy crest be shorn and shaven, thou,' I said, 'art sure no
    craven,
Ghastly grim and ancient Raven wandering from the Nightly
    shore –
Tell me what thy lordly name is on the Night's Plutonian shore!'
              Quoth the Raven, 'Nevermore.'

Much I marvelled this ungainly fowl to hear discourse so plainly,
Though its answer little meaning – little relevancy bore;
For we cannot help agreeing that no living human being
Ever yet was blessed with seeing bird above his chamber door –
Bird or beast upon the sculptured bust above his chamber
    door,
            With such name as 'Nevermore'.

But the Raven, sitting lonely on the placid bust, spoke only
That one word, as if his soul in that one word he did outpour.
Nothing farther then he uttered – not a feather then he
    fluttered –
Till I scarcely more than muttered 'Other friends have flown
    before –
On the morrow he will leave me, as my hopes have flown
    before.'
            Then the bird said 'Nevermore.'

Startled at the stillness broken by reply so aptly spoken,
'Doubtless,' said I, 'what it utters is its only stock and store
Caught from some unhappy master whom unmerciful Disaster
Followed fast and followed faster till his songs one burden
    bore –
Till the dirges of his Hope that melancholy burden bore
            Of 'Never – nevermore.'

But the Raven still beguiling all my fancy into smiling,
Straight I wheeled a cushioned seat in front of bird, and bust
  and door;
Then, upon the velvet sinking, I betook myself to linking
Fancy unto fancy, thinking what this ominous bird of yore –
What this grim, ungainly, ghastly, gaunt, and ominous bird of
  yore
              Meant in croaking 'Nevermore.'

This I sat engaged in guessing, but no syllable expressing
To the fowl whose fiery eyes now burned into my bosom's
  core;
This and more I sat divining, with my head at ease reclining
On the cushion's velvet lining that the lamp-light gloated o'er,
But whose velvet violet lining with the lamp-light gloating o'er,
              She shall press, ah, nevermore!

Then, methought, the air grew denser, perfumed from an unseen
  censer
Swung by Seraphim whose foot-falls tinkled on the tufted floor.
'Wretch,' I cried, 'thy God hath lent thee – by these angels he
  hath sent thee
Respite – respite and nepenthe from thy memories of Lenore;
Quaff, oh quaff this kind nepenthe and forget this lost Lenore!'
              Quoth the Raven 'Nevermore.'

'Prophet!' said I, 'thing of evil! – prophet still, if bird or devil!
Whether Tempter sent, or whether tempest tossed thee here
  ashore,
Desolate yet all undaunted, on this desert land enchanted
On this home by Horror haunted – tell me truly, I implore –
Is there – is there balm in Gilead? – tell me – tell me, I
  implore!'
              Quoth the Raven 'Nevermore.'

'Prophet!' said I, 'thing of evil! – prophet still, if bird or devil!
By that Heaven that bends above us – by that God we both
    adore –
Tell this soul with sorrow laden if, within the distant Aidenn,
It shall clasp a sainted maiden whom the angels name Lenore –
Clasp a rare and radiant maiden whom the angels name Lenore.'
              Quoth the Raven 'Nevermore.'

'Be that word our sign of parting, bird or fiend!' I shrieked,
    upstarting –
'Get thee back into the tempest and the Night's Plutonian shore!
Leave no black plume as a token of that lie thy soul hath spoken!
Leave my loneliness unbroken! – quit the bust above my door!
Take thy beak from out my heart, and take thy form from off my
    door!'
              Quoth the Raven 'Nevermore.'

And the Raven, never flitting, still is sitting, still is sitting
On the pallid bust of Pallas just above my chamber door;
And his eyes have all the seeming of a demon's that is dreaming,
And the lamp-light o'er him streaming throws his shadow on
    the floor;
And my soul from out that shadow that lies floating on the floor
              Shall be lifted – nevermore!

Julian Barnes

1946-

J ULIAN BARNES recalls, in an article he wrote in *The Guardian* on 5th March 2005, visiting three main Flaubert sites in Rouen when he was on holiday in Normandy in 1981.

'First a statue in the intimate and leafy Place des Carmes, where the novelist is looking loftily upwards with a sticking-out moustache, disdaining the game of boules being played beneath him. Next, a walk down the Avenue Flaubert ... to the Flaubert Museum at the Hôtel-Dieu where the novelist's father had been head surgeon. Here, I noted antique medical instruments and family memorabilia, and then most memorably, the bright green, perky-eyed parrot which was lent to him when he was writing *Un Coeur Simple* and which irritated him at the same time as giving him an inner sense of parrothood.

'Finally, a day or two later, I went downstream from the city centre to Croisset and the high point of pilgrimage, the small, square pavilion which was all that remains of the master's house.

'Then, crouched on top of one of the display cabinets, what did we see but *another* parrot. Also bright green, also, according to the *gardienne* ... the authentic parrot borrowed [by Gustave Flaubert when he wrote *Un Coeur Simple*]. I ask the *gardienne* if I can take it down and photograph it. She concurs, even suggests I take it off the glass case. I do, and it strikes me as slightly less authentic than the other one; mainly because it seems benign and Flaubert wrote of how irritating the other one was to have on his desk. As I am looking for somewhere to photograph it, the sun comes out – this on a cloudy, grouchy, rainy morning – and slants across the display cabinet. I put it there and take two sunlit photos;

then, as I pick the parrot up and replace it, the sun goes in. It felt like a benign intervention by Gustave Flaubert – signalling thanks for my presence, or indicating that this was indeed the true parrot.'

Thus Julian Barnes devised his narrator: a retired English doctor who returns to the Normandy beaches as well as to Rouen. He then began at first writing a freestanding short story, but then moved towards something more elastic – a bit of fact and fiction. This excerpt from what became an enormously popular novel recites the musings of the author's hero on Flaubert's life, and his own, as he tracks the stuffed parrot that once inspired the great writer.

Julian Barnes was born in Leicester, England on 19th January 1946. He was educated at the City of London School and at Magdalene College, Oxford. He worked as a lexicographer for the *Oxford English Dictionary* for three years, and then began working as a reviewer and literary editor for the *New Statesman* and the *New Review*. From 1979 to 1986 he worked as a television critic, first for the *New Statesman* and then for the *Observer*. He has written ten novels, two books of short stories and two collections of essays. He has also received several awards and honours for his writings. *Flaubert's Parrot* was short-listed for the Booker Prize in 1984.

Flaubert's Parrot

SIX NORTH AFRICANS were playing boule beneath Flaubert's statue. Clean cracks sounded over the grumble of jammed traffic. With a final, ironic caress from the fingertips, a brown hand dispatched a silver globe. It landed, hopped heavily, and curved in a slow scatter of hard dust. The thrower remained a stylish, temporary statue: knees not quite unbent, and the right hand ecstatically spread. I noticed a furled white shirt, a bare forearm and a blob on the back of the wrist. Not a watch, as I first thought, or a tattoo, but a coloured transfer: the face of a political sage much admired in the desert.

Let me start with the statue: the one above, the permanent, unstylish one, the one crying cupreous tears, the floppy-tied, square-waistcoated, baggy-trousered, straggle-moustached, wary, aloof bequeathed image of the man. Flaubert doesn't return the gaze. He stares south from the place des Carmes towards the Cathedral, out over the city he despised, and which in turn has largely ignored him. The head is defensively high: only the pigeons can see the full extent of the writer's baldness.

This statue isn't the original one. The Germans took the first Flaubert away in 1941, along with the railings and door-knockers. Perhaps he was processed into cap-badges. For a decade or so, the pedestal was empty. Then a Mayor of Rouen who was keen on statues rediscovered the original plaster cast – made by a Russian called Leopold Bernstamm – and the city council approved the making of a new image. Rouen bought itself a proper metal statue in 93 per cent copper and 7 per cent tin: the founders, Rudier of

93

Châtillon-sous-Bagneux, assert that such an alloy is guarantee against corrosion. Two other towns, Trouville and Barentin, contributed to the project and received stone statues. These have worn less well. At Trouville Flaubert's upper thigh has had to be patched, and bits of his moustache have fallen off: structural wires poke out like twigs from a concrete stub on his upper lip.

Perhaps the foundry's assurances can be believed; perhaps this second-impression statue will last. But I see no particular grounds for confidence. Nothing much else to do with Flaubert has ever lasted. He died little more than a hundred years ago, and all that remains of him is paper. Paper, ideas, phrases, metaphors, structured prose which turns into sound. This, as it happens, is precisely what he would have wanted; it's only his admirers who sentimentally complain. The writer's house at Croisset was knocked down shortly after his death and replaced by a factory for extracting alcohol from damaged wheat. It wouldn't take much to get rid of his effigy either: if one statue-loving Mayor can put it up, another – perhaps a bookish party-liner who has half-read Sartre on Flaubert – might zealously take it down.

I begin with the statue, because that's where I began the whole project. Why does the writing make us chase the writer? Why can't we leave well alone? Why aren't the books enough? Flaubert wanted them to be: few writers believed more in the objectivity of the written text and the insignificance of the writer's personality; yet still we disobediently pursue. The image, the face, the signature; the 93 per cent copper statue and the Nadar photograph; the scrap of clothing and the lock of hair. What makes us randy for relics? Don't we believe the words enough? Do we think the leavings of a life contain some ancillary truth? When Robert Louis Stevenson died, his business-minded Scottish nanny quietly began selling hair which she claimed to have cut from the writer's head forty years earlier. The believers, the seekers, the pursuers bought enough of it to stuff a sofa.

I decided to save Croisset until later. I had five days in Rouen, and childhood instinct still makes me keep the best until last. Does the same impulse sometimes operate with writers? Hold off, hold off, the best is yet to come? If so, then how tantalising are the unfinished books. A pair of them come at once to mind: *Bouvard et Pécuchet*, where Flaubert sought to enclose and subdue the whole world, the whole of human striving and human failing; and *L'Idiot de la faille*, where Sartre sought to enclose the whole of Flaubert: enclose and subdue the master writer, the master bourgeois, the terror, the enemy, the sage. A stroke terminated the first project; blindness abbreviated the second.

I thought of writing books myself once. I had the ideas; I even made notes. But I was a doctor, married with children. You can only do one thing well: Flaubert knew that. Being a doctor was what I did well. My wife … died. My children are scattered now; they write whenever guilt impels. They have their own lives, naturally. 'Life! Life! To have erections!' I was reading that Flaubertian exclamation the other day. It made me feel like a stone statue with a patched upper thigh.

The unwritten books? They aren't a cause for resentment. There are too many books already. Besides, I remember the end of *L'Education sentimentale*. Frédéric and his companion Deslauriers are looking back over their lives. Their final, favourite memory is of a visit to a brothel years before, when they were still schoolboys. They had planned the trip in detail, had their hair specially curled for the occasion, and had even stolen flowers for the girls. But when they got to the brothel, Frédéric lost his nerve, and they both ran away. Such was the best day of their lives. Isn't the most reliable form of pleasure, Flaubert implies, the pleasure of anticipation? Who needs to burst into fulfilment's desolate attic?

I spent my first day wandering about Rouen, trying to recognise parts of it from when I'd come in 1944. Large areas were bombed and shelled, of course; after forty years they're still patching up the Cathedral. I didn't find much to colour in the monochrome memories. Next day I drove west to Caen and then north to the beaches. You follow a series of weathered tin signs, erected by the Ministère des Travaux Publics et des Transports.

This way for the Circuit des Plages de Débarquement: a tourist route of the landings. East of Arromanches lie the British and Canadian beaches – Gold, Juno, Sword. Not an imaginative choice of words; so much less memorable than Omaha and Utah. Unless, of course, it's the actions that make the words memorable, and not the other way round.

Graye-sur-Mer, Courseulles-sur-Mer, Ver-sur-Mer, Asnelles, Arromanches. Down tiny sidestreets you suddenly come across a place des Royal Engineers or a place W. Churchill. Rusting tanks stand guard over beach huts; slab monuments like ships' funnels announce in English and French: 'Here on the 6th June 1944 Europe was liberated by the heroism of the Allied Forces.' It is very quiet, and not at all sinister. At Arromanches I put two one-franc pieces into the Telescope Panoramique (Très Puissant 15/60 Longue Durée) and traced the curving morse of the Mulberry Harbour far out to sea. Dot, dash, dash, dash went the concrete caissons, with the unhurried water between them. Shags had colonised these square boulders of wartime junk.

I lunched at the Hôtel de la Marine overlooking the bay. I was close to where friends had died – the sudden friends those years produced – and yet I felt unmoved. 50th Armoured Division, Second British Army. Memories came out of hiding, but not emotions; not even the memories of emotions. After lunch I went to the museum and watched a film about the landings, then drove ten kilometres to Bayeux to examine that other cross-Channel invasion of nine centuries earlier. Queen Matilda's tapestry is like horizontal cinema, the frames joined edge to edge. Both events seemed equally strange: one too distant to be true, the other too familiar to be true. How do we seize the past? Can we ever do so? When I was a medical student some pranksters at an end-of-term dance released into the hall a piglet which had been smeared with grease. It squirmed between legs, evaded capture, squealed a lot. People fell over trying to grasp it, and were made to look ridiculous in the process. The past often seems to behave like that piglet.

On my third day in Rouen I walked to the Hôtel-Dieu, the hospital where Gustave's father had been head surgeon, and where the writer spent his childhood. Along the avenue Gustave Flaubert, past the Imprimerie Flaubert and a snack-bar called Le Flaubert: you certainly feel you're going in the right direction. Parked near the hospital was a large white Peugeot hatchback: it was painted with blue stars, a telephone number and the words AMBULANCE FLAUBERT. The writer as healer? Unlikely. I remembered George Sand's matronly rebuke to her younger colleague. 'You produce desolation,' she wrote, 'and I produce consolation.' The Peugeot should have read AMBULANCE GEORGE SAND.

At the Hôtel-Dieu I was admitted by a gaunt, fidgety *gardien* whose white coat puzzled me. He wasn't a doctor, a *pharmacien* or a cricket umpire. White coats imply antisepsis and clean judgment. Why should a museum caretaker wear one – to protect Gustave's childhood from germs? He explained that the museum was devoted partly to Flaubert and partly to medical history, then hurried me round, locking the doors behind us with noisy efficiency. I was shown the room where Gustave was born, his eau-de-Cologne pot, tobacco jar and first magazine article. Various images of the writer confirmed the dire early shift he underwent from handsome youth to paunchy, balding burgher. Syphilis, some conclude. Normal nineteenth-century ageing, others reply. Perhaps it was merely that his body had a sense of decorum: when the mind inside declared itself prematurely old, the flesh did its best to conform. I kept reminding myself that he had fair hair. It's hard to remember: photographs make everyone seem dark.

The other room contained medical instruments of the eighteenth and nineteenth centuries: heavy metal relics coming to sharp points, and enema pumps of a caliber which surprised even me. Medicine then must have been such an exciting, desperate, violent business; nowadays it is all pills and bureaucracy. Or is it just that the past seems to contain more local colour than the present? I studied the doctoral thesis of Gustave's brother Achille: it was called 'Some Considerations on the Moment of Operation on the Strangulated Hernia'. A fraternal parallel: Achille's thesis later became Gustave's metaphor, 'I feel, against the stupidity of my time, floods of hatred which choke me. Shit rises to my mouth as in the case of a strangulated hernia. But I want to keep it, fix it, harden it; I want to concoct a paste with which I shall cover the nineteenth century, in the same way as they paint Indian pagodas with cow dung.'

The conjunction of these two museums seemed odd at first. It made sense when I remembered Lemot's famous cartoon of Flaubert dissecting Emma Bovary. It shows the novelist nourishing on the end of a large fork the dripping heart he has triumphantly torn from his heroine's body. He brandishes the organ aloft like a prize surgical exhibit, while on the left of the drawing the feet of the recumbent, violated Emma are just visible. The writer as butcher, the writer as sensitive brute.

Then I saw the parrot. It sat in a small alcove, bright green and perky-eyed, with its head at an inquiring angle. '*Psittacus*,' ran the inscription on the end of its perch: 'Parrot borrowed by G. Flaubert from the Museum of Rouen and placed on his work-table during the writing of *Un cœur simple*, where it is called Loulou, the parrot of Félicité, the principal character in the tale.' A Xeroxed letter from Flaubert confirmed the fact: the parrot, he wrote, had been on his desk for three weeks, and the sight of it was beginning to irritate him.

Loulou was in fine condition, the feathers as crisp and the eye as irritating as they must have been a hundred years earlier. I gazed at the bird, and to my surprise felt ardently in touch with this writer who disdainfully forbade posterity to take any personal interest in him. His statue was a retread; his house had been knocked down; his books naturally had their own life – responses to them weren't responses to him. But here, in this unexceptional green parrot, preserved in a routine yet mysterious fashion, was something which made me feel I had almost known the writer. I was both moved and cheered.

On the way back to my hotel I bought a student text of *Un cœur simple*. Perhaps you know the story. It's about a poor, uneducated servant-woman called Félicité, who serves the same mistress for half a century, unresentfully sacrificing her own life to those of others. She becomes attached, in turn, to a rough fiancé, to her mistress's children, to her nephew, and to an old man with a cancerous arm. All of them are casually taken from her: they die, or depart, or simply forget her. It is an existence in which, not surprisingly, the consolations of religion come to make up for the desolations of life.

The final object in Félicité's ever-diminishing chain of attachments is Loulou, the parrot. When, in due course, he too dies, Félicité has him stuffed. She keeps the adored relic beside her, and even takes to saying her prayers while kneeling before him. A doctrinal confusion develops in her simple mind: she wonders whether the Holy Ghost, conventionally represented as a dove, would not be better portrayed as a parrot. Logic is certainly on her side: parrots and Holy Ghosts can speak, whereas doves cannot. At the end of the story, Félicité herself dies. 'There was a smile on her lips. The movements of her heart slowed down beat by beat, each time more distant, like a fountain running dry or an echo disappearing; and as she breathed her final breath she thought she saw, as the heavens opened for her, a gigantic parrot hovering above her head.'

The control of tone is vital. Imagine the technical difficulty of writing a story in which a badly-stuffed bird with a ridiculous name ends up standing in for one third of the Trinity, and in which the intention is neither satirical, sentimental, nor blasphemous. Imagine further telling such a story from the point of view of an ignorant old woman without making it sound derogatory or coy. But then the aim of *Un Cœur simple* is quite elsewhere: the parrot is a perfect and controlled example of the Flaubertian grotesque.

We can, if we wish (and if we disobey Flaubert), submit the bird to additional interpretation. For instance, there are submerged parallels between the life of the prematurely aged novelist and the maturely aged Félicité. Critics have sent in the ferrets. Both of them were solitary; both of them had lives stained with loss; both of them, though full of grief, were persevering. Those keen to push things further suggest that the incident in which Félicité is struck down by a mail-coach on the road to Hornfleur is a submerged reference to Gustave's first epileptic fit, when he was struck down on the road outside Bourg-Achard. I don't know. How submerged does a reference have to be before it drowns?

In one cardinal way, of course, Félicité is the complete opposite of Flaubert: she is virtually inarticulate. But you could argue that this is where Loulou comes in. The parrot, the articulate beast, a rare creature that makes human sounds. Not for nothing does Félicité confuse Loulou with the Holy Ghost, the giver of tongues.

Félicité + Loulou = Flaubert? Not exactly; but you could claim that he is present in both of them. Félicité encloses his character; Loulou encloses his voice. You could say that the parrot, representing clever vocalisation without much brain power, was Pure Word. If you were a French academic, you might say that he was *un symbole du Logos*. Being English, I hasten back to the corporeal: to that svelte, perky creature I had seen at the Hôtel-Dieu. I imagined Loulou sitting on the other side of Flaubert's desk and staring back at him like some taunting reflection from a funfair mirror. No wonder three weeks of its parodic presence caused irritation. Is the writer much more than a sophisticated parrot?

We should perhaps note at this point the four principal encounters between the novelist and a member of the parrot family. In the 1830s, during their annual holiday at Trouville, the Flaubert household regularly used to visit a retired sea-captain called Pierre Barbey; his ménage, we are told, included a magnificent parrot. In 1845 Gustave was travelling through Antibes, on his way to Italy, when he came across a sick parakeet which merited an entry in his diary; the bird used to perch carefully on the mudguard of its owner's light cart, and at dinnertime would be brought in and placed on the mantelpiece. The diarist notes the 'strange love' clearly evident between man and pet. In 1851, returning from the Orient via Venice, Flaubert heard a parrot in a gilt cage calling out over the Grand Canal its imitation of a gondolier: '*Fà eh, capo die.*' In 1853 he was again in Trouville; lodging with a *pharmacien*, he found himself constantly irritated by a parrot which screamed, '*As-tu déjeuné, Jako?*' and '*Cocu, mon petit coco.*' It also whistled '*J'ai du bon tabac.*' Was any of these four birds, in whole or in part, the inspiration behind Loulou? And did Flaubert see another living parrot between 1853 and 1876, when he borrowed a stuffed one from the Museum of Rouen? I leave such matters to the professionals.

I sat on my hotel bed; from a neighbouring room a telephone imitated the cry of other telephones. I thought about the parrot in its alcove barely half a mile away. A cheeky bird, inducing affection, even reverence. What had Flaubert done with it after finishing *Un cœur simple*? Did he put it away in a cupboard and forget about its irritating existence until he was searching for an extra blanket? And what happened, four years later, when an apoplectic stroke left him dying on his sofa? Did he perhaps imagine, hovering above him, a gigantic parrot – this time not a welcome from the Holy Ghost but a farewell from the Word?

'I am bothered by my tendency to metaphor, decidedly excessive. I am devoured by comparisons as one is by lice, and I spend my time doing nothing but squashing them.' Words came easily to Flaubert; but he also saw the underlying inadequacy of the Word. Remember his sad definition from *Madame Bovary*: 'Language is like a cracked kettle on which we beat out tunes for bears to dance to, while all the time we long to move the stars to pity.' So you can take the novelist either way: as a pertinacious and finished stylist; or as one who considered language tragically insufficient. Sartreans prefer the second option: for them Loulou's inability to do more than repeat at second hand the phrases he hears is an indirect confession of the novelist's own failure. The parrot/writer feebly accepts language as something received, imitative and inert. Sartre himself rebuked Flaubert for passivity, for belief (or collusion in the belief) that one *est parlé* – one is spoken.

Did that burst of bubbles announce the gurgling death of another submerged reference? The point at which you suspect too much is being read into a story is when you feel most vulnerable, isolated, and perhaps stupid. Is a critic wrong to read Loulou as a symbol of the Word? Is a reader wrong – worse, sentimental – to think of that parrot at the Hôtel-Dieu as an emblem of the writer's voice? That's what I did. Perhaps this makes me as simple-minded as Félicité.

But whether you call it a tale or a text, *Un Cœur simple* echoes on in the brain. Allow me to cite David Hockney, benign if unspecific, in his autobiography: 'The story really affected me, and I felt it was a subject I could get into and really use.' In 1974 Mr Hockney produced a pair of etchings: a burlesque version of Félicité's view of Abroad (a monkey stealing away with a woman over its shoulder), and a tranquil scene of Félicité asleep with Loulou. Perhaps he will do some more in due course.

On my last day in Rouen I drove out to Croisset. Normandy rain was falling, soft and dense. What was formerly a remote village on the banks of the Seine, backdropped by green hills, has now become engulfed by thumping dockland. Pile-drivers echo; gantries hang over you, and the river is thickly commercial. Passing lorries rattle the windows of the inevitable Bar le Flaubert.

Gustave noted and approved the Oriental habit of knocking down the houses of the dead; so perhaps he would have been less hurt than his readers, his pursuers, by the destruction of his own house. The factory for extracting alcohol from damaged wheat was pulled down in its turn; and on the site there now stands, more appropriately, a large paper-mill. All that remains of Flaubert's residence is a small one-storey pavilion a few hundred yards down the road: a summer house to which the writer would retire when needing even more solitude than usual. It now looks shabby and pointless, but at least it's something. On the terrace outside, a stump of fluted column, dug up at Carthage, has been erected to commemorate the author of *Salammbô*. I pushed the gate; an Alsatian began barking, and a white-haired *gardienne* approached. No white coat for her, but a well-cut blue uniform. As I cranked up my French I remembered the trademark of the Carthaginian interpreters in *Salammbô*: each, as a symbol of his profession, has a parrot tattooed on his chest. Today the brown wrist of the African boule-player wears a Mao transfer.

The pavilion contains a single room, square with a tented ceiling. I was reminded of Félicité's room: 'It had the simultaneous air of a chapel and a bazaar.' Here too were the ironic conjunctions – trivial knick-knack beside solemn relic – of the Flaubertian grotesque. The items on display were so poorly arranged that I frequently had to get down on my knees to squint into the cabinets: the posture of the devout, but also of the junk-shop treasure-hunter.

Félicité found consolation in her assembly of stray objects, united only by their owner's affection. Flaubert did the same, preserving trivia fragrant with memories. Years after his mother's death he would still sometimes ask for her old shawl and hat, then sit down with them to dream a little. The visitor to the Croisset pavilion can almost do the same: the exhibits, carelessly laid out, catch your heart at random. Portraits, photographs, a clay bust; pipes, a tobacco jar, a letter opener; a toad-inkwell with a gaping mouth; the gold Buddha which stood on the writer's desk and never irritated him; a lock of hair, blonder, naturally, than in the photographs.

Two exhibits in a side cabinet are easy to miss: a small tumbler from which Flaubert took his last drink of water a few moments before he died; and a crumpled pad of white handkerchief with which he mopped his brow in perhaps the last gesture of his life. Such ordinary props, which seemed to forbid wailing and melo-drama, made me feel I had been present at the death of a friend. I was almost embarrassed: three days before I had stood unmoved on a beach where close companions had been killed. Perhaps this is the advantage of making friends with those already dead: your feelings towards them never cool.

Then I saw it. Crouched on top of a high cupboard was another parrot. Also bright green. Also, according to both the *gardienne* and the label on its perch, the very parrot which Flaubert had borrowed from the Museum of Rouen for the writing of *Un cœur simple*. I asked permission to take the second Loulou down, set him carefully on the corner of a display cabinet, and removed his glass dome.

How do you compare two parrots, one already idealised by memory and metaphor, the other a squawking intruder? My initial response was that the second seemed less authentic that the first, mainly because it had a more benign air. The head was set straighter on the body, and its expression was less irritating than that of the bird at the Hôtel Dieu. Then I realised the fallacy in this: Flaubert, after all, hadn't been given a choice of parrots; and even this second one, which looked the calmer company, might well get on your nerves after a couple of weeks.

I mentioned the question of authenticity to the *gardienne*. She was, understandably, on the side of her own parrot, and confidently disclaimed the claims of the Hôtel-Dieu. I wondered if somebody knew the answer. I wondered if it mattered to anyone except me, who had rashly invested significance in the first parrot. The writer's voice – what makes you think it can be located that easily? Such was the rebuke offered by the second parrot. As I stood looking at the possibly inauthentic Loulou, the sun lit up that corner of the room and turned his plumage more sharply yellow. I replaced the bird and thought: I am now older than Flaubert ever was. It seemed a presumptuous thing to be; sad and unmerited.

Is it ever the right time to die? It wasn't for Flaubert; or for George Sand, who didn't live to read *Un cœur simple*. 'I had begun it solely on account of her, only to please her. She died while I was in the midst of this work. So it is with all our dreams.' Is it better not to have the dreams, the work, and then the desolation of uncompleted work? Perhaps, like Frédéric and Deslauriers, we should prefer the consolation of non-fulfilment: the planned visit to the brothel, the pleasure of anticipation, and then, years later, not the memory of deeds but the memory of past anticipations? Wouldn't that keep it all cleaner and less painful?

After I got home the duplicate parrots continued to flutter in my mind: one of them amiable and straightforward, the other cocky and interrogatory. I wrote letters to various academics who might know if either of the parrots had been properly authenticated. I wrote to the French Embassy and to the editor of the Michelin guide-books. I also wrote to Mr Hockney. I told him about my trip and asked if he'd ever been to Rouen; I wondered if he'd had one or other of the parrots in mind when etching his portrait of the sleeping Félicité. If not, then perhaps he in his turn had borrowed a parrot from a museum and used it as a model. I warned him of the dangerous tendency in this species to posthumous parthenogenesis. I hoped to get my replies quite soon.

Christopher Ondaatje

1933-

ALTHOUGH CHRISTOPHER ONDAATJE's literary career since 1988 has focused mainly on accounts of his adventures in Africa and South-East Asia, more recently he has concentrated on articles and short stories for magazines in the United Kingdom, the United States and Asia. These magazines have been hungry for personal and unusual experiences. He has been lucky, because he has much to write about, but he has also found out that short story writing in itself is a most difficult form. Let's face it, there are very few really good short stories in the world. John Steinbeck, the great American writer, said that a story to be effective has to convey something from the writer to the reader, and the power of its offering is the measure of its success. But the author must also know what he is talking about. One exercise Steinbeck recommends is to try to reduce the meat of the story to a single sentence, because only then could one know the subject well enough to expand it to three, or six, or ten thousand words. 'If there is magic in story writing, and I am convinced there is,' Steinbeck says 'no one has ever been able to reduce it to a recipe that can be passed from one person to another. The formula seems to lie solely in the aching urge of the writer to convey something he feels important to the reader.'

Christopher Ondaatje's story 'The White Crow' seems to have broken all the rules, but it is based on fact. It is certainly unusual and possibly unbelievable. But strange things happen in the East and events that seem strange to Westerners are often not quite so strange to those living in countries where demonology and witchcraft are very much part of everyday life.

The White Crow

ONE OF THE strangest afternoons I have ever spent in Colombo was with the late President J.R. Jayawardene (1906-1996) three years before he died. He was an extraordinary man, the first Executive President of Sri Lanka (1978-1989), and the man singly responsible for changing the constitution of the country to a Gaullist system which introduced an executive presidency. A man with immense power, he was not above criticism, particularly for not acting swiftly to prevent Sinhalese mobs attacking Tamils in a frenzy of ethnic violence in July 1983. These attacks led to an intensification of the separatist struggle by militant Tamil groups, notably the L.T.T.E. (Liberation Tiger of Tamil Eelam), and the emigration of many Tamil families. Increased military pressure of the insurgents, who had been receiving help from India, brought Indian intervention. The L.T.T.E. rejected Jayawardene's 1988 Accord which agreed to devolve power to a North-Eastern Provincial Council to meet Tamil demands for autonomy and turned against a newly formed Indian Peace Keeping Force (I.P.K.F.) sent by Delhi to force the L.T.T.E. to disarm. He retired in 1989 while the L.T.T.E. and the I.P.K.F. were still battling, with the ethnic problem no nearer a solution.

When I last met J.R. Jayawardene in 1993, I was in Sri Lanka helping the historian Hendrik Hooft publish, first in Dutch and then in English, his epic biography *Patriot and Patrician*, which followed the steps in Holland and Ceylon of our ancestors Hendrik Hooft and Pieter Ondaatje, who were champions in the 1780s of a popular movement which brought to the Dutch Republic the first democratically elected government in Europe, a few years before the French Revolution.

Jayawardene was also a great romantic, student of history, and a superb raconteur. At tea at his home in Ward Place, after showing us around his Jayawardene Centre on Turret Road, he held us enthralled with his recollections of Queen Elizabeth II's visit to Ceylon in 1981. 'How would you like your people to see me?' the Queen asked the President. 'I think they would like to see you with your crown on, Your Majesty,' Jayawardene replied. 'I'm sorry, Mr President, but I don't travel with my crown,' the Queen apologised. Later the Queen had told the President that her most embarrassing moment had been in Uganda during a state visit in 1954 when, in a private and intimate moment, four hundred school children had burst into 'God Save the Queen'.

However, this is not the story I intended to relate. As anyone who has driven along, or entered one of the spacious houses that line the treed avenue of Ward Place, it is difficult not to notice the noisy armies of crows that inhabit the trees and gardens in the area. They are large birds, over a foot long, with heavy pointed bills and powerful legs. Omnivorous, they eat fruit, large insects, small vertebrates, as well as other birds' eggs and young. Often seen on the ground, I know from experience that they are extremely intelligent birds, gregarious and noisy as a rule, and are entirely black with a very slight metallic sheen.

Therefore it was not so surprising that as 'Henk' Hooft and I were driven with the former President in his limousine, past the guarded gates to the portico in front of the President's house, that we noticed several crows busily and collectively going about their activities in the President's garden. However, what was surprising, and both of us noticed it without comment, was one crow, entirely white in colour except for its pink legs and a light grey beak – an extraordinary sight. The white crow seemed also to be the leading instigator of the other crow activities.

Intent on listening to what President Jayawardene was telling us during the drive, I said nothing further until much later in the afternoon when we had had sandwiches and tea, and were thinking of leaving. Indeed the President had moved to the window overlooking his garden and seemed himself engrossed in watching the activities of the crows on his garden lawn. Seizing my moment, I moved next to him and asked about the curious presence of the white crow. He paused pensively for a few minutes, turned to me and said, 'I think we had better sit down.'

Moving away from the window, the President, quite serious now in his outlook, looked at us and asked me, 'What do you know about Meredith Foster? Do you remember, a few years ago, the British press announced the disappearance of the English reporter who had come to Sri Lanka in the mid 1980s to cover the eruption of the violence against the Tamil minority here. It was a terrible time for us, and a particularly difficult time for me because I had to make some very difficult decisions to try to stem the Sinhalese mob violence. Not everything worked, even with the Indian Peace Keeping Force help. In fact, the strained argument between the Sinhala and Tamil population became intensified with the unpopular Indian involvement. Anyway, Miss Foster's reports, and I say Miss Foster although I realise she had a husband in England, got world-wide attention for a while – particularly in the Western world. She was a good writer, seemed to have a better than average understanding of a complicated political situation, and took some quite extraordinary risks to get her stories – sometimes actually going to battle fronts and war zones where reporters were definitely not allowed. She made quite a name for herself overseas, but also here in Colombo where she was based and where she spent most of her time when she was not in the field. Her husband did visit her occasionally at first but she really seemed to have made a permanent home for herself in the Barnes Place area, also in Colombo 7, not far from here.

'I suppose she was here for six or seven years before she suddenly went missing – supposedly on one of her more dangerous reporting missions. There was terrible consternation because both the Tigers and the Sri Lankan army had taken great pains to advise and protect foreign journalists – knowing full well the bad press this troubled island would get if a Western reporter was hurt or killed. But for a long time there was some confusion as to Miss Foster's whereabouts and her reporting mission. And then over the next few months, with no further news, the mysterious situation died down and there was little or no further press.'

I did remember news in England about the disappearance of an English reporter. It caused quite a stir at the time, but I said nothing as President Jayawardene seemed anxious to continue his story.

'Well, what the foreign press and few people knew, was that Meredith Foster, a good looking blonde girl in her mid-thirties, was known by all of us close to the government to be having rather a serious affair with a high ranking official in the government. It certainly was an embarrassment for all of us, but nothing was done about it although the minister in question – a married man himself – was warned several times about the dangers of the compromising relationship. The situation was further complicated because the minister's wife was herself related to the Bandaranaike family and we knew she was understandably in a high state of anxiety about her husband's involvement. We knew there would be trouble sometime.

'Now, I want to ask you a very personal question. Do you know anything about Demonology and Witchcraft?' We both shook our heads, never taking our eyes off the President's face. He was eager to continue.

'Well, Sri Lanka, together with Haiti and South Africa, is known to be among the most sophisticated in the practice of demon worship. The belief in the realities of an invisible world of evil spirits has not always received an acceptance in most parts of the Western world, but in this country superstition, coupled with the worship of gods and demons, as well as Buddhism, has had an extraordinary degree of influence on the minds of the Sinhala people. Even respected historians and writers, from Robert Knox in the 17th century, and more recently Sir Emerson Tennant, have written of the results of their enquiries and experiences in matters connected with this island. Curiously, Buddhism acknowledges the probable existence of demons and tolerates, even if it does not openly countenance the practice of demon-worship, or at least a good deal of what belongs to it. A Sinhala demon is himself a being subject to death, like all other beings recognised by Buddhism, although that event may in some instances take place only at the end of some tens of thousands of years. This difference arises from the Buddhist doctrine that there is no state of perpetual existence for any being: that happiness or misery can never be perpetual; that the rewards or punishments for the actions of one life will be reaped in one or more states of existence afterwards and then come to an end; and that mere obedience to a demon does not necessitate any disobedience to one's religion.

'The priests of demonism are styled *Yakaduras*, *Yakdessas*, or more commonly *Cattadiyas*, and there is scarcely a village in the island which does not boast of at least one. So it is not that surprising that when someone gets into trouble, or is involved in a relationship or situation which cannot be resolved in a normal way of life, that they ask advice and put themselves in the hands of a village *Cattadiya* – who can call on one of the demons or malignant *Yakseyo*, who are invisible but do have the power to make themselves visible, generally in some other shape, often that of beasts, or of men, or of women. There are many of these demons and they are said to have enormous influence over life, death, disease, health and love. Although it is believed that there are a great many demons in existence, the number of those who belong to demon worship does not exceed fifty or sixty, and there are a great many books and letters on the subject. This is a complicated business involving *Hooniyan* charms, *Agarm* and *Pilli* charms, and even *Jæwang* charms whose object is to bind any demon in a certain manner so as to make the demon an obedient slave to its master. There are many, many learned books and letters on the subject – many not yet translated from the Sinhala language.

'You must also try to understand that *Cattadiyas* or priests receive no particular respect from anyone as the Buddhist priest does. The village priest's profession is looked upon as any ordinary calling, like a shopkeeper or boatman. There is nothing sacred about him like a Buddhist priest, and his main job is to cure or inflict diseases and other tasks by the agency of demons. There are many of them. For example *Reeri Yakseya*, the demon of blood, who is considered to be the most cruel and powerful; *Calu Cumara Dewatawa* or the Black Prince particularly exposes young and fair women to his attacks; and *Madana Yakseniyo* is the name given to the seven sisters or female demons of lust. Then there is *Baddracali*, a demon whose assistance is sought for winning lawsuits and for subduing enemies and rivals of any kind; and it may be that the wife of the government official with whom Meredith Foster was intimately involved called on *Baddracali* to help her in solving her matrimonial problem – of course through the agency of her village *Cattadiya* in her home town near Kandy.

'But there is also *Bahirawa Yakseya*, another female demon generally feared for being able to inflict diseases on women, and it is to *Bahirawa Yakseya* that we now think that the government official's wife called on through her priest – mainly because *Bahirawa Yakseya* is known to have operated on a giant hill, *Bahirawa Canda*, which you may know and which stands looking over one side of the town of Kandy. Remember she comes from that area, and residents of the Kandy region have been steeped in folklore of *Bahirawa Yakseya*, who is known to have influenced one of the earlier Queens of Kandy, who was pregnant and who also was known to have miscarried several times within a few months of her confinement. Eventually, and again through the agency of a village *Cattadiya*, the demon categorically stated that he would not remove her influence over the Queen unless a yearly sacrifice of a young virgin was made to her on the summit of *Bahirawa Canda*. The King of Kandy, hearing this, did as he was told and after that several children were born to his young wife.

'Now it is suspected, and I only know this by hearsay, that the politician's wife was told by the demon that in order to rid herself of Meredith Foster and save her marriage she must sacrifice her rival in the same way that the sacrifices were made for the Queen of Kandy: a stake being driven into the ground on the summit of *Bahirawa Canda*, the girl tied to it with jungle creepers, flowers, and boiled rice placed close by on an altar constructed for the purpose; and certain invocations and incantations pronounced to conclude the ceremony. Inevitably, the next morning the girl would be found dead. Thus it was, we suspect, that Meredith Foster, during one of her many assignments, was kidnapped and taken to *Bahirawa Canda* in Kandy and tied to the sacrificial stake. Her body was never seen again.

'The strange thing about this story is that there is living today an old woman in Kandy who was also offered up to the demon in an earlier life, during the reign of Sri Wikreme Rajasingha, the last King of Kandy. But somehow or other she managed to effect her escape. When questioned further, she explained that the demon *Bahirawa Yakseya*, although having considerable powers over disease, did not in fact have any power over life and death, which is why the demands were made for the young virgin to be sacrificed in such a gruesome manner. Inevitably, it is true, the next morning the young girl would be found dead – not from any direct propitiation by the demon but almost certainly from either exposure or fright. The old woman further explained that escape was possible in only two different ways – either by reincarnation, as she had chosen, where she could choose to take the form of a human in another life, in another time, or take on the immediate form of an animal or bird of the demon's choosing and approval.

'Nobody really knows what happened, but this female white crow appeared here in Ward Place almost eight years ago, at almost exactly the same time that Meredith Foster disappeared. No one talks about it much because Sri Lankans, as I explained, are extremely superstitious and fear reprisals from a slate of demons if they are ever suspected of any thoughts or deeds questioning the actions of any spirit. Of course many people come, with permission, to see the strange albino-like bird, but they say nothing. It flies off to other gardens and busy streets, where it is sometimes seen, but people are very careful not to disturb or frighten it in any way, and certainly not to harm it. And it always returns here, where it congregates with other crows, seeming sometimes even to be their charismatic leader.'

What an incredible story! Neither 'Henk' Hooft nor I had very much to say. We just stared in disbelief at what President Jayawardene had just told us. But then, almost at the moment that we were making our excuses and thanks, and preparing to depart, we heard a continuous and persistent tapping on the drawing room window overlooking the garden at 66 Ward Place. Looking towards the irritating noise we were amazed to see that it was the white crow, which was on the other side of the window sill, continuing to tap on the glass with its beak, as if giving some kind of a message in code. President Jayawardene then, completely unfazed, got up in his flowing white Ariya Sinhala costume, for he was indeed a stately figure of a man, walked slowly and purposefully to the window and opened it. Immediately the white crow flew into the drawing room, circled briefly around the centre, and then alighted on the President's shoulder, quite as if it knew exactly what was expected of it. The President too seemed completely at ease with what had just happened.

I was just about to say something when I saw the President looking at me with a threatening expression. We stared at each other for a few brief moments. He said nothing. Nothing needed to be said. With a half apologetic smile on his face he shrugged slightly, not disturbing the lovingly possessive bird.

Richard Francis Burton

1821-1890

*F*ALCONRY IN THE VALLEY *of the Indus* was the fourth of Richard Burton's books to be published after his return to England in 1849 after seven years in India. Only 500 copies were printed of this rare masterpiece, and I treasure my own as among my most prized possessions. Burton commented about the book, 'It was brought out by my friend, John Van Voorst... He proved himself to be a phoenix among publishers. "Half profits are no profits to the author" is the common saying; however, for the last thirty years I have continually received from him small sums, which represented my gains. Would that all were so scrupulous!' This small book is more than a description of hunting with falcons in Sindh. It is also an opportunity for Burton to portray some of the characters he was beginning to meet in his travels. His portrayals show him to be capable of the acute anthropological observations for which he became famous. As always, he flings himself into this introduction to falcony in Sindh with all the passion of a lover. It is a wonderfully instructive document that can scarcely contain the author's enthusiasm for one of the oldest hunting sports in the world.

Richard Francis Burton was born on 19th March 1821 in Hertfordshire, England, son of Colonel Joseph Netterville Burton. His youth was spent on the Continent where, with his brother Edward and his sister Maria, he enjoyed what can only be regarded as a highly irregular education at the hands of servants and schoolmasters who were shocked at the boys' high spirits and apparent inability to obey any rules. He did, however, excel at duelling, riding, shooting, gambling and experimenting with anything he'd been forbidden to try. His father sent him to Trinity College, Oxford where he showed a remarkable talent for languages. But his time at Oxford ended in infamy when he was sent down for demonstrating outstanding insubordination. He then joined the army of the British East India Company and from the moment he set foot in Bombay, India was a revelation to him. Despite the strictures of army life, he threw himself fully into the mysteries of the East, concentrating on pleasure, knowledge, Eastern erotica, native languages and religion. He explored the farthest regions of the Sindh desert, often in disguise.

One of his assignments in Sindh, however, appears to have led to the premature end of his army career. General Charles Napier assigned Burton to investigate the boy brothels of Karachi. Some time after Burton completed the assignment his report reached army authorities, who were shocked at its content and who assumed that Burton's detailed descriptions could only have been achieved through his own participation in what he was describing. Whatever the truth, Burton was shipped back to England.

After a short recuperation, he set off on a lifetime of further adventures. He entered Mecca in disguise in 1853; he fought in Somaliland; he searched for the source of the Nile in 1855 and 1857-58; he crossed America to be among the Mormons of Salt Lake City. In 1861 he was posted as a diplomat to Fernando Po, an island off Africa. By that time he had married Isabel Arundel, who was to remain his faithful companion for decades to come. He was posted to Santos, Brazil in 1865, to Damascus in 1869, and finally, in 1872, to Trieste where he and Isabel lived out the years remaining until his death in 1890.

Burton's writing career, which culminated in his famous translation of the *Arabian Nights*, spans his entire life from India onward. His first book, *Goa, and the Blue Mountains* was published in 1851; *Scinde, or the Unhappy Valley* was also published in 1851, as was Burton's most significant contribution to the recording of Sindh's culture, *Sindh, and the Races that inhabit the Valley of the Indus*.

'The Untimely Death of Khairu the Hobby' is a unique story extracted from his fourth book, *Falconry in the Valley of the Indus*. Burton's descriptions of his hunting experiences and his evocation of the hawks and falcons, and indeed his delineation of the language and technique of falconry, bring this sensitive story to life.

The Untimely End of Khairu the Hobby

W E – THAT IS TO SAY, my friend Ibrahim Khan Talpoor, with Kakoo Mall his secretary, and I, supported by Hari Chand, – were passing the last of an active day's hours spent amongst the marshes, in our reed armchairs, under the spreading Neem trees of the Ameer's village. Behind us lay my modest encampment, a tent or two, half a dozen canvas sheds, tenanted by government Khalassis;[1] horses picketed in their night clothes, camels at squat, apparently ruminating on many a grievance; 'Pepper', the terrier, looking even more spiteful than usual, because tied up to prevent his polluting the garments of the Faithful,[2] and motley little groups of Scindian beaters, Hindoo chainmen and rodmen, Affghan 'horse-keepers', and Brahui camel-men, scattered about in all directions. Conspicuous among them stood Antonio the Portuguese butler, in the dignity of a jacket, and Gaetano, his *aide-de-camp*, with a face like a mandril's, a shirt distended to a balloon shape by the evening breeze, and a striped calico pantaloon *collant*, taut drawn as the wet leathers into which an Oxford buck of the last generation used to be shaken and packed by the united force of his scout and groom.

Directly in front of us, so placed that they could enjoy a full view of our every movement, sat a semi-circle of the Ameer's retainers, smoking, conversing and listening to the words of wisdom that fell

1 Tent-pitchers, surveying assistants, &c.
2 The touch of a dog being impure to the Moslem.

121

from our lips, as gravely as a British jury empanneled on a matter of life and death.

It was a fine December evening in Scinde, very like the close of a fine May day in England. The western sky was blushing rosy red as it received the sun into its bosom, the gentle breeze felt cool and sounded crisp, light mists began to float on the distant horizon, and over the uninteresting forms of the foreground, lay a veil of purple light and reddish shade, that forced the eye to linger upon them with pleasure. In fine, the view before us was a mass of common-place beauty which the oftener we see the more we learn to admire and love.

A purling rill, artificial, but to be mistaken for natural, coursed within a few yards of our feet on its way towards a little stuccoed cistern, in the midst of the Ameer's jujube garden. Over it stood the Neem trees, throwing thick shades from their emerald arms, and rustling in the evening breeze with a sweet melancholy significance.

At such an hour – in such a scene – could Oriental gravity fail to fall into pensiveness, into that terrible habit of moralizing in which Orientals love to indulge?

'Ah!' said the Ameer, 'how happily might not one spend one's life under a tree like that,' pointing to a peculiarly tall one, 'only, however, taking care to put mats round it by way of walls. How long one would last! and how much one would eat!'

The time was after dinner: the Ameer's sentiment a remarkable one for that time. Hari Chand and Kakoo Mall (who both had dined) uttered their 'Wah Wahs!'[3] but looked at each other furtively, and methought, with *goguenard* glances. The idea of living under green wood was that of a Jat.[4]

'The Neem tree!' exclaimed Kakoo, who felt bound to support his patron, 'justly is it called the Azad Darakht[5] – the free tree – it

3 Bravos!
4 A gipsy, or wild man.
5 Hence the botanical name of the tree, *melia azadirachta*; the leaves made up into balls are swallowed as an antidote to the venom of the cobra.

blooms eternally like the doer of good works' – (Kakoo, remember, was a notable scoundrel); – 'and it bears no fruit, like the man of God whose harvest is not in this life.'

The Ameer was affected, so was the crowd; each man mentally comparing Kakoo and his own picture of the *melia azadirachta*, detrimentally to the former.

'Verily, yes,' responded Hari; 'and it profits the world in its generation; its leaves are an antidote to the poison of snakes, even as content is to the gnawings of worldliness' – (Hari was at least as bad as Kakoo); — 'besides, its twigs are useful as tooth-sticks.'[6]

'But not equal to those of the Arak,'[7] broke in the Ameer; 'our blessed Prophet used these, therefore should every true Moslem do the same. However, ye say truth, the Neem tree is a Fakir.'

'About which,' pursued Hari Chand, 'the poet sang –

"Man's nature alters not;

The Neem remains bitter, though you water it with milk and honey."'

We were jogging very prettily, I began to think, along the beaten track of Oriental conversation, when our course was arrested by an unforeseen incident.

Instead of the occasional cawings and croakings of crows, to which the ear of the Indian traveller by habit speedily becomes deaf, suddenly arose such a din of corvine voices, such shrieks and such a clashing of wings above and around us, that not one of the conversationists or the listeners but that turned his head.

The crow is a kind of sacred bird amongst the Hindoos, which fact accounts, in some degree, for his uncommon impertinence. He is fed at certain seasons with boiled rice and other delicacies, so that he never, at any time, can witness the operation of cooking with the slightest attempt at patience. I have seen him again

---

6   Orientals use a stick chewed to softness at one end, instead of the European toothbrush.
7   A kind of Salvadora, common in Arabia, Persia and Scinde (where it is called Khabbar), &c.

and again swoop at a dog and carry off a bone which he persuades the hungry brute to drop, by a sharp application of his stout, pointed bill upon its muzzle. At times I have expected to be attacked myself by the friends and relations of the deceased, when, after half an hour's dance with St. Vitus to the tune of some villanous old scout's croak, I disposed of the musician by an ounce of shot. And if you wish to enjoy a fine display of feathered vicious-ness, order your servant to climb up a tree full of crows, and to rob the nearest nest. At such seasons it is as well to stand by with a loaded gun or two, otherwise the sport might end in something earnest to the feather-less biped.

The reason of the row was soon explained. Gaetano had thoughtlessly left a half-plucked chicken preparing for my supper within sight of a sentinel crow, whose beat was the bough of a neighbouring Neem tree. In a moment it was pounced upon, seized, and carried off. On one side all the comrades of the plunderer flocked together to share in the spoils which he resolved to appropriate, and most violent was the scene that ensued. On the other, up rushed the cook, the butler, the Khalassis, and all the horse-keepers, as excited as the crows, determined to recover with sticks and stones the innocent cause of the turmoil.

'Send in for Khairu, the Laghar,' said the Ameer, in a whisper-ing voice to Kakoo, as if afraid of being overheard by some listen-ing crow. He certainly thought that if he spoke loud the birds would recognize the name, and really after some study of their idiosyncrasy, I did not treat the precaution of his tone lightly. Aesop had no experience in the character of the Indian 'Kak',[8] otherwise he would not have made the Fox outwit the Crow.

One of the attendants rose slowly from the ground, and look-ing indifferently around him, went off by a *detour* towards the palace.

Presently appeared two men dressed in green, with a large sheet spread between their shoulders so as to cover their near arms.

8 *Kawla*, or *kawwa*, a crow.

Behind them came the attendants carrying a dozen pellet and other bows.

The pellet-bow merits a short description; – it would be a prodigious acquisition in Europe to naughty little boys who delight in breaking their neighbours' windows. It is made of a slip of bamboo, bent in the shape of our ancient weapon; as the old proverb advises, it has two strings stretched parallel to each other from horn to horn. About the centre a bit of canvas or coarse cloth, an inch or an inch and a half in length, is sewn tightly to the two cords, and against it the pellet, a lump of hard clay, about the size of a 'taw', is firmly held by the thumb and forefinger, which draw the bow.

By dint of practice the natives of India can use this instrument upon small birds with fatal effect: the range is from sixty to eighty yards. To a tyro the only inconvenience of it is the occasional smashing of the pellet upon the thumb knuckle of the left hand, an event quite the reverse of agreeable, and which invariably brings on a repetition of itself, in consequence of Tyro's nervous anxiety to avoid it.

The sight of these preparations for destruction in the servants' hands elicited one long loud caw from every crow that happened to be looking that way. Instantly those that were on the wing began skeltering in headlong flight through the foliage of the trees towards some safer roosting-place, and the few that were perched, sprang up, flapping and shrieking, and following with all speed the example of their fellows. Even the chicken was forgotten in the hurry of the moment.

'Let the bone of contention lie under the tree, and if we don't notice them some will be back shortly,' said the Ameer. 'Take Khairu into the tent and hide the bows.'

The veteran falconer was right. About ten minutes afterwards an old crow was descried sneaking behind the plantation, and silently taking up a position in the thickest cover he could find. Then came a second and third; at last, we were aware of the presence of a dozen.

'Bring the bird,' whispered the Ameer.

The Bazdar[9] came softly out of the tent, carrying on his fist Khairu, the Laghar,[10] who was sitting erect, as if mentally prepared for anything, with head pressed forward, and pounces[11] firmly grasping the Dasti.[12] Her hood was then removed, her leash was slowly slipped, and as one crow bolder than the others lit furtively upon the ground, where the half-plucked chicken lay, Khairu, cast off with a whoop, dashed unhesitatingly at the enemy.

Another tumult. Every Beloch, that could handle a bow, provided himself with one, and all of us hurried to the open space whence we could descry the evolutions of the birds.

At the sight of the hawk, the crow precipitately dropped his prize, and shrieking as usual, skurried through the trees pursued by *his* stubborn foe.

Now all is excitement. The attendants rush about whooping and hallooing, in order if possible to frighten the quarry still more. Vainly the crow attempts to make a distant shelter, the Laghar hangs close upon him, gaining every moment. Corvus must shift *his* tactics. Now he attempts to take the air, wheeling in huge circles gradually contracted. But Khairu has already reached his level, another instant a swoop will end the scene. The crow falls, cunningly as might be expected; presenting his bill and claws he saves himself from the stoop, and having won, as he supposes, distance, cleverly turns over, and wriggles through the air towards his asylum. Already it is near – a large clump of thorny mimosas, from whose rugged boughs resound the voices of a startled colony. Khairu, with a soldier's glance, perceives the critical moment, plies her pinions with redoubled force, grapples with her quarry from behind, weighs him down rapidly through the cleaving air, and

---

9 Falconer.
10 'Laghar', a large kind of hobby-hawk.
11 The 'pounces', in the language of falconry, are the bird's talons.
12 Oriental falconers, instead of a glove, use a small square napkin of wadded cotton, secured to the wrist by a noose, and twisted round the hand so that the bird sitting on the forefinger may clench it with her talons.

nearing the earth, spreads her wings into parachute form, lighting with force scarcely sufficient to break an egg.

The battle is not finished. Corvus, in spite of *his* fall, his terror, a rent in the region of the back, and several desperate pecks, still fights gallantly. Ibis is the time for the falconer to assist his bird. From the neighbouring mimosas, roused by the cries of their wounded comrade, pours forth a 'rabble rout' of crows, with noise and turmoil, wheeling over the hawk's head, and occasionally pouncing upon her, *unguibus et rostris*, with all the ferocity of hungry peregrines. We tremble for Khairu. Knowing her danger, we hurry on, as fast as our legs can carry us, shouting, shooting pellets, and anathematizing the crows. We arrive, but hardly in time. As we plunge through the last bushes which separate us from the hawk, twenty cawers rise flurriedly from the ground: the Bazdar hurries to his Laghar. The quarry lies stone dead, but poor Khairu, when taken up and inspected by thirty pair of eyes, is found to have lost her sight, and to be otherwise so grievously mauled, pecked, and clawed, that the most sanguine prepare themselves for her present decease.

Alas, poor Khairu!

'I never yet heard of good coming from these accursed Kang,'[13] said the Ameer as we slowly retraced our way towards the encampment; 'one of them I am sure killed my poor brother at Meeanee. All the night a huge black crow sat upon the apple of his tent pole, predicting the direst disasters to him. We drove away the beast of ill-omen half a dozen times, still he would return.'

'Yet,' Kakoo Mall ventured to observe, 'the crow of the wild, the *Ghurab el bain*, is frequently commended by the poets as a Mujarrad,[14] and even they make him their messenger when sending a mental missive to those they love.'

'They are asses, and sons of asses! and thou, O Kakoo! art the crow of all the Kafirs!' responded Meer Ibrahim Khan, angrily: 'have not these, thy kinsfolk, killed Khairu, the Laghar?'

13 A crow in the Scinde tongue.
14 One detached from the pomps and vanities, &c.